Jay caught Maria from behind. As she opened the door he grabbed her around the neck and pulled her back inside the apartment. Even though he had her neck, he didn't stop her from screaming until he got her back into the apartment. He didn't even remember sticking the long bladed knife into her back. When she fell back into his arms blood gushed from the back wound, covering his hands and arms. The checkered white jacket he wore was covered with blood from the sleeves onward.

The other two men in the apartment didn't even realize that Jay had stabbed the woman until she screamed over and over again, "George, George, he's killing me!"

—CRY REVENGE

Donald Goines

CRY REVENGE

HOLLOWAY HOUSE PUBLISHING COMPANY
LOS ANGELES, CALIFORNIA

PUBLISHED BY
Holloway House Publishing Company
8060 Melrose Avenue
Los Angeles, California 90046
International Standard Book Number 0-87067-069-7
Printed in the United States of America

DEDICATION

A friend indeed will help a friend in need. So saying, I'd like to say my thanks to some friends of mine who have helped me while others turned their backs. At the top of the list is Levern Sawyer and his wonderful wife Pearl. Next I'd like to thank Brother Auther, or better known as Deek Reed. Also on the long list would be Kenneth Heggerman and his Lady Rickie. Last but not least, I'd like to say thank you to Frank Usher, better known to his friends as Frank Nitty. While these are not all of the people, they are some of my closest friends, or rather people I'm proud to think of as my personal friends.

1

IN THE BACK YARD of the white frame house was sand. Brown, light sand, that blew in from the distant desert. New Mexico was more desert than anything else, yet it still possessed a beauty that would be hard to find elsewhere.

Curtis Carson stood up and put his hands on his hips as he shook out the kinks in his back. He stared down at the dice that his friend Dan Lewis shook.

"Seven!" Dan yelled, as he rolled the dice out. He snatched them back up quickly as eight showed. "Seven," he yelled again, this time taking his time and trying to roll the dice gently on the sand. Again the dice came up showing an eight.

"These mothafuckers ain't got nothin' on them but eights," Dan cursed loudly. Then he shook the dice slowly, holding them back near his ear. He grinned up at Curtis who picked up the money he had made after jumping eight. "Now," Dan yelled, "I want to see some fuckin' sevens on these mothahuppas."

The two Mexican men kneeling in the dirt watched Dan closely as he shook the dice. The stouter of the two tossed his money down beside Dan's. "Okay, momma," he said, drawing the words out, "you're faded."

Dan stared down at the ten dollar bill laying in the dirt. He grinned up at the men, revealing good teeth that needed some cleaning. "Now that's the way I like to get my money on, with no problems." He took his time, then quickly released the dice. The dice hit the dirt and began to spin around like small tops.

Before the dice could stop spinning, the Mexican who had faded the money reached over and snatched the dice up from the dirt. "Goddamn, Dannie, how many times we got to go over it! Ain't goin' be no spinning the dice in the sand!"

"The sonofabitch," the other Mexican said, loud enough for all the men in the game to hear. "The gringo bastard must think we are the fools, huh?"

"Hey, amigo," Curtis said smoothly, "sometimes people forget, you know. Ain't nobody been hurt, the dice were caught, so let's not get nasty about it, okay?" His voice had remained low, but there was no doubt about the authority in it. The tall Black was used to giving orders.

The slim Mexican who had spoken glanced up from his kneeling position. "Hey, my man, how many times do we have to pull this dude's coat about tryin' to shoot that shot on us, huh?"

Curtis shrugged his wide shoulders. "These things happen, Pedro, you're hip to it. The guy is used to firin' the craps that way, so all at once we want him to change his style of shootin' cause you guys say he's gettin' slick. So the guy tries and changes his style of shootin', but at times he forgets, you know, and goes back to firin' the craps the way he's used to shootin' them. That's all it is."

Pedro glared up at Curtis, but prudence warned him not to push it. He glanced around and caught his partner's eyes, then glanced down at the money in the pot. His actions were obvious to everybody in the game.

Before the other Mexican could pick his money up out of the dirt, Dan picked up the dice and rolled them out. "Seven, baby," he yelled, as the craps slowly rolled across the dirt.

Before the heavy-set Mexican could follow his partner's directions, the dice had rolled out and stopped on a seven. Pedro let out a curse and glared angrily at the dice shooter.

"Seven, and we have a winner," Curtis yelled

out, making it clear to the angry Mexicans that it had been a fair roll.

Pedro coughed and cleared his throat. "Yeah, Dannie boy, you really think you're cute, don't you, my man?" His jet black eyes were flashing dangerously as he tried to control his temper.

Dan, a tall, slim brown-skinned man in his early twenties smiled coldly. Though his lips were pulled back in a smile, his dark eyes were bleak and deadly as he watched the Mexican out of the corner of them.

"Hey Pedro," he called out softly, "what's the deal man? You say I'm tryin' to be cute. I can't dig that, brother. I'm just tryin' to win some cash money, that's all, my man."

Before Pedro could say anything, his partner punched him in the side with his elbow. "It's okay, dude, you caught me with my pants down on that roll."

Dan smiled at the heavy-set Mexican. "That's the way I like to hear people rap, Jay. You win some, and you lose some."

Jay Novello, the husky Mexican, ignored Dan as he got up from the crap game. "I think we had better be movin' on, amigo," Jay stated as he reached out and touched the quick-tempered Pedro's arm. "It's nothing, amigo, but a few dollars."

"Hey, brother, wait a minute now. I don't want you to leave with no kind of attitude now, 'cause

by Al C. Clark

ain't nobody did nothin' to you," Curtis stated
sharply, then added, " 'cause if you think you been
cheated, run it down to me. I don't run no kind of
crooked game, not in my momma's back yard no
way." Curtis stepped in front of the two men.
"Now if you got some kind of complaint, let's get
it off your chest when we can clear up the air right
now!"

"We ain't got no complaints, Curtis," Jay stated,
"but we done warned this dude six or seven times
about shootin' that turn-down shot on us, but he
still takes us for tricks."

"Hey, Jay," Curtis replied quietly, "we both saw
the shot he used when he rolled seven just now and
it wasn't no turn-down shot he used. Before, yes,
but you caught the dice, Jay, so now what the fuck
is the problem?" Before Jay could answer, Curtis
went on. "Now, if you're hot over losin' your
money, I ain't about to replace it, so you're shit
out of luck. If you couldn't stand to lose, you
shouldn't have started to gamble!"

His words beat at the two men, each one feeling
the weight of them as he spoke. Pedro glanced
upward at the sky. Jay, on the other hand, glanced
down at his shoes, then moved nervously from one
foot to the other. He slowly raised his eyes and
stared at Curtis.

"Hey, amigo, we ain't fools, you dig? Now I
been beat out of a few dollars," Jay began, speaking with slow deliberation and looking directly into

11

Curtis' eyes. "But the money ain't about nothin', Curtis. What hurts, amigo, is that we thought we were more cooler with you than that." Jay raised his hand, cutting off whatever Curtis was about to say. "I know without it being said, that we been hustled, Curtis, but that ain't about shit. What I'm tryin' to say is, I thought we were tighter than that, but it's okay, my man. Them things happen. Maybe you needed the few dollars that your main man won, who knows, I don't, and I don't give a fuck!"

Curtis frowned, but didn't say anything. He listened quietly as the Mexican continued to speak.

"We ain't got no attitude, as you said, Curtis, we just didn't think you'd hustle us." Jay shrugged, looking like an overgrown bulldog at that moment—his pug nose quivering, his black eyes sparkling.

After much shifting about, Pedro managed to get into the conversation. "Yeah, Curtis, we never figured you'd turn on us like that, man. It ain't like it should be. Friends ain't supposed to play on each other, not when they're cool with each other."

Finally Dan got tired of listening to the two complaining Mexicans. "Hey, what kind of shit is this," he began. "Before you guys get carried away, why don't you dig this sho' nuff shit. It wasn't none of Curtis who ripped you off. It was me, so why the fuck are you wasting your time wearing his eardrums off. I'm the one who beat you out of your money, so if you think you got played on, take it up with me, not him!"

Pedro shifted suddenly and his hand dipped down to his pocket. Jay's words froze him in that position.

"We ain't got no argument with neither one of you," Jay stated. "We got beat, and that's it!"

"Well," Dan drawled, "I just hope your friend happens to feel the way you do about it, Jay, 'cause if he don't, this motherfuckin' sociable littl' party could turn into somethin' neither one of us want."

Jay attempted to laugh it off, as he gripped Pedro's arm tightly. He could feel the firm muscles tightening and retightening under his fingers. Pedro was quick-tempered, and dangerous as any coiled rattlesnake. His temper was unpredictable and no one knew it better than Jay. At the present moment, though, Jay didn't want any trouble out of the Blacks.

"It ain't about nothing, I said," Jay stated again. This time he gave Pedro a small push and started him toward the side of the house.

Pedro stopped and whirled on his heel. "Hey, Curtis," he began, "I never thought you would sock it to me like that, man."

Curtis folded his arms across his wide chest. "No comprendo, Pedro, my man. I just don't know where you're coming from. But before we fall out

13

over a littl' money, I'd rather kick back your money and keep your friendship." But Curtis didn't make any move toward his pocket.

For a second Pedro just stared at him. "I just bet you will," he replied, his cold black eyes never leaving the face of the tall Black man he spoke to.

Suddenly Curtis laughed, a cold chilling sound without any mirth in it. "Hey, my man, I'm going to pull your coat one more time, Pedro, then you can take it any way you want to. This is my mother's pad, man, so I wouldn't start any shit around here, and sure nuff don't want any kind of troubles. So you should be able to understand that."

Seeing that the shit was about to get deep again, Jay didn't waste any time. "Hey amigo," he said lightly as he took Pedro's arm and turned him back around. This time he didn't try and be gentle. "I said it was all right, Pedro, so forget it man, you dig?"

"If you say so, Jay," Pedro answered, "but I ain't about to forget about it."

"Do whatever the fuck you want to do!" Curtis stated sharply.

Dan rubbed his chin as he watched the two Mexicans depart. "You know, Curt, we might have some trouble out of them spics, brother."

Curtis shook his head. "I doubt it. If it was one of the other Fernandez brothers, I'd say yes, but our boy Pedro is a blowhard. He's quick-tempered

by Al C. Clark

as hell, but he also forgets shit. He won't even think about it this time tomorrow."

"You think he's going to pull his brother's coat that we bumped his head?" Dan inquired.

Again Curtis shrugged his wide shoulders. "It's hard to say, Dan. Right now his pride is hurt, so no tellin'. If he didn't think he was the smartest bastard in the world it would be easy to figure him out, but since he don't think like other people, I don't know. First of all, he might not want his brothers to know that he was foolish enough to start shooting craps in my back yard. His pride might not allow him to confess his stupidity to others."

"Well I hope you're right, Curt, 'cause if you ain't, we goin' have trouble coppin' some good stuff from them Mexs."

"Well, ain't no sense us worryin' 'bout what we can't help, is there Dan?"

For an answer Dan grinned, then slapped his partner on the back. "Okay, Curt, you know more about these Mexicans than I'll ever be able to find out, so I'll go along with your judgment."

"Good!" Curtis replied, "now let's get on into the pad and see what Mom has got together in that big pot she was cookin' in." Curtis didn't wait for an answer, he led the way toward the back door. He pushed the screen door open and stepped in. The rear porch was crowded with debris. Three large gray ashcans sat near the door that led into

15

the house, while cardboard boxes with various items in them were everywhere. The rear porch was screened in, so that people could sit on the back porch and enjoy the nights without fear of being eaten to death by insects.

At the sound of the two young men walking on the porch, a woman's voice called out, "Curtis, is that you?"

"Yeah, Ma," he answered quickly, as he stopped at the rear door that led into the house and began to wipe his feet off.

"I'm sure glad you boys have finished gambling out there, Curtis," she stated. "You know how much I hate to see you gambling period, let alone in our yard."

Before he could say anything to an old argument of his mother's, she continued. "One of these days you niggers are going to get yourselves killed over one of them cheap dice games. Hell, I'd be surprsied to death if there was over ten dollars in the whole game!"

Both men grinned at each other, then Dan removed the bankroll from his pocket and began to count it. "Shit!" he exclaimed happily, "I believe Jay blowed his whole paycheck." To make sure, he recounted the money in his hand. "Yeah, I won one hundred and fourteen dollars, Curt."

Curtis removed the money from his pocket and quickly counted it. "Good, we got one hundred and fifty dollars between us, Dan. That's more than enough to cop us a good bag of stuff." Curtis held the door open for his friend and partner. "Besides the money, Dan, we got a pot of black-eyed peas waitin' on us inside," he stated, as he lifted his nose and smelled deeply. "Yes sirreee, my nose ain't never fucked around and let me down, man. Whenever I tell you what's smokin' in the pot, brother, you can lay money on it I'm right!"

The two men entered the kitchen which was right off the back porch. Curtis' mother, a large, heavy-set woman, was standing at the stove. She twisted her head around and smiled at the men. When she opened her mouth, the empty spaces where her teeth had been were visible.

"I just know you done trimmed them Mexicans out of their littl' bit of money," she stated as the two men settled down in the center of the kitchen at the small table.

"Now Moms," Curtis began, "we just happened to get lucky today, that's all."

"Shit!" she replied loudly. "If you waited on luck you'd never have a damn thing!" Mrs. Carson said seriously as she waddled away from the stove and made her way across the floor to the white painted cabinet over the kitchen sink. She removed two dishes and carried them back and set them down in front of the men. Her broad black face broke out into a grin as she began to load their plates from a large bowl that had been sitting on the table. She went back to the stove and opened the oven, removed a cornbread pan and cut two large slices and carried them back to each man's plate. Finally, she brought them both large glasses of Koolade and put them on the table.

"Damn!" Dan exclaimed, "I don't know how I'm ever going to get all this food down. Shit, Momma, if I ate at your house every day, I'd weigh over five hundred pounds!"

Mother Carson loved to cook. And next to that, she loved to watch men eat. She prided herself on always having enough, no matter how many friends Curtis or his brother Billy brought home for dinner.

"Where's Billy at?" Curtis inquired as his mother came back to the table, this time carrying some butter in a tray.

Before answering, Mother Carson reached up and wiped the sweat off the red handkerchief she wore wrapped around her head. The bandanna was filthy from long use, while the white apron she wore was almost spotless. Her features were average—for a Black housewife over fifty. She was fat to an excess, revealing that she also loved her own cooking just as much as she liked seeing other people eat it.

"I believe your brother is up to the Center playing basketball," she answered in a voice that matched her size.

"Shit, Billy goin' turn into a goddamn basketball one of these days," Curtis stated offhandedly.

"Better for him to spend his time at the Center playing basketball than running the streets like you and Dan. Ain't no good goin' come of it, you can bet your Black ass on it, too," she said harshly, not bothering to respect the feeling of her sons guest.

"Now Momma," Dan began, but he was cut off sharply.

"Don't 'now momma' me," she said harshly, "I know what you two niggers are up to when you're out in them streets, so don't try and shit me." Her voice rose higher as she spoke until she was nearly shouting.

"Momma," Curtis said softly, trying to change the subject, "now we don't need to go into all that crap today, do we?"

She just snorted, then got up from the table and made her way over to the cabinet. When her back was turned, Curtis motioned for Dan to hurry up and eat. He wanted to get away before his mother started to preach.

Their plates were too heavy for the two men to just gulp the food down, so they were still there when she returned, carrying another clean plate. She sat it down and placed a knife and spoon beside it. The two men could hear what she had heard earlier—someone had entered the front door and was now making their way through the house toward the kitchen.

Suddenly a tall dark-skinned young boy stood in the doorway. He was slim, yet well put together.

His shoulders had the wideness of Curtis', yet he was smaller than his brother. The large shoulders tapered down to a thin waist. From the shorts he wore, you could see the strong legs of the young man. His features were almost identical to those of his older brother. Yet, there was a difference. Where Curtis' eyes were cold and hard, Billy had soft eyes—eyes that were not yet ruined by his surroundings.

His mother's face broke into a wide grin at the sight of him, and it could easily be seen that her young son was held in deep respect.

"The game broke up early today, didn't it?" she inquired as she made a place at the table for him.

Billy nodded his head, then spoke up. "Naw, Moms, we didn't do nothing but practice today, that's all." He nodded at his brother and Dan, not bothering to speak to either of the men.

"Practice, practice, practice," Curtis said coldly. "Don't you ever get tired of firing that ball at the hoop, Billy?"

"Naw, brother, I don't get any more tired than you do of running up and down the alleys searching for a crap game that ya can cheat in!" he drawled not bothering to conceal the sarcasm in his voice. "Why don't you come on back out for the team, Curt. You used to be the best center in the city, man."

"Big deal," Curtis answered, "and when I was the best center in the city, I couldn't even buy a pair of pants to cover my Black ass!"

"Hey, man, everything takes time, Curt, you know that. It was just a matter of time before one of them big colleges gave you a free ride through school. Then after that, shit, man, you could name your own price."

"Yeah, I know. Four fuckin' . . ."

Before he could go any further, he heard his mother's sharp reprimand. "Okay, now, Curtis, I don't need that kind of language in this house and you know it. It just goes to show what you pick up in the streets, Curtis, you don't respect nobody anymore!"

"I'm sorry, Moms", Curtis began, trying to apologize. It just slipped out, that's all. You know I didn't mean no disrespect by it."

"Yeah, Curtis, I know you didn't," she answered slowly, "but that's just what I'm talking about. Those streets teach you them things."

Dan finished his plate of food and pushed it to the middle of the table. Mrs. Carson glanced out of the corners of her eyes to see if he had finished everything. It was wiped clean, so she didn't make any comment.

Curtis followed his friend's action, only his plate wasn't as clean. His mother gave him a cold stare but again didn't make any comment. As the two men got up from the table, she pushed back the seat she had taken and followed them towards the door.

"Curtis," she began as they walked slowly toward the door that led out of the kitchen and into the hallway to the living room, "if you see your sister anywhere, you tell her to get her butt home. It's way past time for her to be home from summer school. Goodness, I don't know which one of you will put me in my grave first, you or Rita!"

As the men walked briskly through the hallway, Curtis didn't bother to answer. He had heard this statement all his life. It seemed as if he was putting his mother in her grave ever since he was a little boy. But even though he didn't mention it to his mother, he'd make sure Rita got her ass home if he saw her on the streets. He hated to see the crowd she ran with. All the girls were easy, and wild as hell.

The freshly painted hallway was long. The three bedrooms in the house were set off from the hallway. Two were on one side, while the other bedroom with the toilet next to it was on the other side. When the men reached the living room, their steps were silenced by the thick carpet. It wasn't wall to wall carpeting but the accumulation of three old rugs piled on top of each other, which gave that effect. The top rug, was reddish and checkered, matching the black couch and chair that took up most of the room. The living room contained a dining room set that no elderly woman would do without in the early sixties. A matching china cabinet with the good dishes were kept there on display.

Mother Carson followed the two men right to the front door. She even held it open as they went out. "Now remember, Curtis, send your sister home if you see her, hear?"

Curtis glanced irritably at his mother, then the feeling died as he saw the worried look in her face. She didn't really mean any harm, but she did get on his nerves with her constant nagging about the so-called dangers of the streets.

"Don't worry, Moms," Curtis replied, then leaned over and kissed her on the cheek. It was something he hadn't done for quite a few years, and he could see the surprise come into her eyes as he removed his arms from around her neck and stepped back. "Just do like I said, Momma, and don't worry. If you want, I'll go out of my way and find her and see to it that she gets her ass home."

As a nod of appreciation came from her, he grinned and caught up with Dan. "Don't worry, Mrs. Carson," Dan called out, "I'll look after both of them for you!" he laughed loudly, and pounded Curtis on the back. Mrs. Carson stood in the doorway and watched the two men make their way down the street. She knew she shouldn't worry, but Curtis reminded her too much of her husband, and it was all too clear in her mind how he had died. As long as she lived, she'd always believe the streets had killed her husband, and every night she prayed to the Lord that the streets wouldn't likewise be the death of her oldest son.

2

DAN AND CURTIS only had to walk three blocks
before they were up on the set. The black-topped
New Mexico street where they hung out consisted
of two poolrooms and four bars, two bars on each
side of the street. Soldiers staggered from one bar
to the next on week-ends, as they sought the few
good-looking whores who worked the bars and the
street corner.

Their first stop was a poolroom where Curtis
inquired about the whereabouts of Fat George, an
old Mexican who was the largest dope dealer on
their side of town. Not seeing Fat George's new
Ford, Curtis knew it would take a while before
George showed up. Since the man hadn't given
Curtis any phone number when they had talked a
few days ago, all he could do was wait and hope

that the Mexican would show up some time that evening.

"What do you think?" Dan inquired, as the two men came out of the first poolroom and walked slowly towards the next one.

"What do I think about what?" Curtis asked, vacantly, letting his thoughts wander.

"About George, that's what. Do you think he's going to show up, or what?" Dan asked, not letting it drop.

His mind still wandering, Curtis gave a shrug, then he stopped suddenly in the street. "I'll bet that silly little bitch is hanging out over at the Do-Drop-Inn!"

"Maybe," Dan replied. "Ain't but one way to find out for sure, though." Both men started walking down the street. The Do-Drop-Inn was a restaurant and bar, but it didn't sell whiskey. Only beer and wine, the specialty being a large pitcher of draft beer that was a favorite of most of the customers. The age limit was supposed to be eighteen and up but the owner, Joe, allowed the young girls in the neighborhood to come in. The boys were another case. If a dude couldn't show proof that he was eighteen he wouldn't be allowed inside the place. Some boys who were really old enough to get in still had trouble if they didn't have their identificcation on them when Joe asked for it.

The bar was located in the middle of the block, across the street from one of the poolrooms. The first thing that reached the two men as they entered the club was the loud sound of the juke-box. Curtis had to blink his eyes before they became accustomed to the darkness of the place. The restaurant part of the club was in the front. Tables were set up in the middle of the floor, while neat rows of booths were along the wall. To reach the club part where the drinking and dancing went on, a customer had to walk to the rear of the club and enter through the back door. It was just one step down and then you were in the part where the dancing and drinking went on. Again, booths lined the wall, while small tables filled the rest of the club. There was no bar, only a large dance area in the middle of the floor. When a customer ordered a pitcher of beer, the waitress had to walk over to the window that opened into the kitchen. There was a woman standing there whose only job was taking the orders from either one of the three waitresses who stayed busy delivering the drinks to the tables.

Now as Curtis glanced around the club, he could see the place was crowded with soldiers from the nearby base. They came in at all hours of the day to dance and try and make it with the young girls who sometimes skipped school so that they could hang out at the Do-Drop-Inn.

"Over there," Dan said, and pointed at a booth in the rear of the club. As Curtis followed Dan's direction he saw a group of young girls and two soldiers packed together in the booth. In the dimness of the club, it was hard to make them out. But as Curtis stared, he heard the high laughter of one of the girls and he knew then that he had found Rita. There was no mistaking her loud laughter. No one laughed the same way she did.

Curtis led the way towards the rear of the club. As they neared the booth, Rita saw her brother coming and began to get up from the table. Ordinarily Curtis didn't interfere with what she did, so she was surprised to see him coming toward her.

The owner of the club, Joe, watched from his private table next to the dance floor. He knew Curtis by sight, and he knew Curtis' sister was under age. The last thing he wanted was any kind of trouble out of some angry brother—not over any young girl. It was too easy for him to lose his license, even though he paid the police off regularly.

Before Rita and Curtis met, Joe was up and moving his huge bulk toward them. As he drew near he overheard Curtis say, "Your momma is worried about you, Rita, so you better get on home and see what she wants."

"Shit!" Rita exploded, revealing at once that she had had too much beer to drink. "I ain't no child, Curt, so I don't know why the hell you're going out of your way to run me down."

At first, Curtis was surprised by her reply, then anger welled up inside of him. "Hey, Sis, this is

Curt, your big brother, not one of these phony ass niggers you mess around with down here, so don't give me any of your shit, I don't want to hear it!"

"Well," she said, pouting, "I ain't in no hurry to go home, so you just run along and take care of whatever business you got to take care of!"

Joe stared at the tall, brown-skinned girl with the short mini-skirt. He'd wished many a time that he could've gotten into her drawers. Big legs and large tits, though her facial features were more mannish than he'd have liked. She had a short natural hair style that made her resemble a man even more, while her nose was short and blunt. Her eyes were the same as her brothers', jet black, with heavy eyebrows. She had the same height that the men in her family had, standing almost six feet tall without shoes. And while wearing the latest style, the huge heels, she towered over six feet. Still, one could see she was still young and had some more growing to do. When she smiled, she revealed evenly spaced white teeth. But there was something cruel about her. It could be seen in her face—a cattish look. Yet many men would still think she was very lovely.

Now as she spoke, there was nothing lovely about her. Her lips were formed into a sneer. "I ain't in no hurry, Curt, to go home and hear no fuckin' preaching," she said, putting her hands on her hips.

Before Joe could interfere, Curtis' hand came up

in a blur and he slapped her viciously across the face. One of the soldiers jumped up from the table where he had been watching the byplay between the two.

"You just hold onto that fuckin' seat," Joe warned. Curtis, I don't need that kind of shit in here, so you get your sister on out, but no more slaps, okay?"

Curtis stared coldly at the fat black man. At first he wanted to give Joe a hard time, but quickly realized that the owner of the club was right.

The slap had brought Rita to her senses, she knew she had pushed her brother too far, and she had no intention of pushing him any further. He must have been mad about something else, she reflected, because he rarely put his hands on her. It had been years since he has last slapped her.

"Damn, Curt," she moaned softly, "you didn't have to do that."

"I just don't want to hear any of your smart lip, Rita," he said, beckoning toward the door. "Now let's get the hell out of here."

Dan glared at the soldier who still wanted to come to the girl's rescue, not so much to really help her, but because she had drank up so much of his beer and he had hoped to get the tall black girl into the nearest motel. Now, she was being led away by her brother, so the money he had spent on her was all wasted.

Dan stepped back and let Rita walk past him. He

couldn't help but admire the large ass she had. With the miniskirt riding high on her hips, he got a good look at what he liked to see. If she ever bent over, he reflected, she'd have to show her natural ass. The skirt was so short that just the slightest bend in her back would reveal the color of the drawers that she wore.

No one spoke until they were on the sidewalk in front of the Do-Drop-Inn. It had been Curtis' plan to walk her home, but as they reached the street, the first thing he saw was Fat George pulling up in his late model Ford. Dan spotted him at the same time.

"Looks like we're running in luck," Dan stated.

"Rita," Curtis began, "I want you to take your ass on home, now. I ain't going to follow you, but I mean for you to go there, you dig?" He waited a second, then added, "I'll be there in about fifteen minutes, so I want to see you when I get there. Now you can act cute if you want to and not go home, but whenever I find you, I'm going to kick the living shit out of you! You understand where I'm coming from?"

"Naw," she answered harshly, "I don't know where you're coming from, but I'll do what you say." She hesitated for a second, then added, "Curt, I don't know what's buggin' you, bro, but I don't dig this shit of yours coming down on me like I'm your whore or something."

"Well that's too damn bad," he replied, "but

you ain't but sixteen, so if you give me any trouble I'll personally see to it that Joe don't let you in his joint no more."

The threat of being kept out of Joe's was enough to make her change her ways quickly. Joe's was the only place in town for young girls to really have fun. Other than that she'd have to go over to her girlfriend's house to dance, and that was really boring. Their parents would be watching, and none of them allowed their young daughters to bring any soldiers home. It was the same with her mother. She wouldn't allow a soldier in the house. She thought the soldiers would try and take advantage of her daughter.

If there was one thing Rita didn't want, it was her brother telling her mother that she was with some soldiers. She might have to stay home for a week or two before she'd be allowed back out on the streets.

"Aw Curt," she began, pleading openly, "you and me ain't never had no misunderstanding that we couldn't rap about, Bro. I'm sorry if I said anything out of the way back there, but I been drinkin' a littl' too much beer, that's all. I got myself together now, so ain't we still cool with each other?" She flashed him her most pleasing smile, showing the well-kept teeth that she was so proud of.

Curtis had to smile in return. "Don't worry, Rita, I ain't goin' to do no tattletelling this time, just as long as you do like I said and take your fat ass home."

Rita started walking in the direction of their house, waving back over her shoulder at her brother. "Bring me a pop when you come home," she called back as she continued on her way.

Trying not to be observed, Dan watched the young girl walk away. Her legs were bowed just enough to give her that real sexual look as she walked. Wide-legged, her young hips swayed smoothly with each long step she took.

"She's too young for you, Dan," Curtis stated as he caught the look on his partner's face.

"Hey, my man, you don't think I'd have any thoughts in that direction, would you? Shit, Curt, I look at Rita as if she's my young sister or something, man."

"Yeah, I just bet you do," Curt replied slowly. "From the way you were digging her ass, I'd hate to see what you would do to your own sister!"

"Aw man," Dan said, guilt all over his face, "I'm sorry you think that a way."

"Forget it," Curtis replied, as he began to lead the way towards the parked car. As they neared the Ford, a large, heavy-set Mexican came out of the bar and stopped on the sidewalk. He spoke jokingly with the people lounging in front of the club.

"What it is?" Curtis stated as they neared the man, "I hear you're gettin' all the money in town,

George." Fat George turned and smiled in his direction.

"What's happenin', Curtis? Who you and Dan been rippin' off lately?" George asked as the men came up on the sidewalk.

Both men grinned at the so-called big man as they neared him. "How about takin' us over on Hill Street, we got somethin' to pick up you might like," Curtis asked as they stopped in front of George.

Fat George caught on at once. "Hey, man, you know I ain't no taxi, but this time I'll do it for you two guys, 'cause you're all right with me." George spoke loudly for the benefit of the idle loafers in front of the bar.

Anything that was said would be repeated a hundred times after the men left. The loafers didn't have anything else to do but meddle in other peoples' business. Their lives were wasted, most of them would never get any farther than Main Street in New Mexico. They would spend their whole lives in useless loafing in front of one bar or another. Then sometimes you'd find them piled inside someone's car, drinking and laughing.

The door on the passenger side of the car was locked, so Curtis and Dan had to stand on the sidewalk and wait until George got in and unlocked the door. Before they pulled off, one of the loafers came away from the store front and walked in front of the car. He came around to the drivers' side. George let his window down quickly, removing the bored expression that flashed across it.

"Yeah, Hip Daddy," George said to the small black man who approached the car, "what can I do for you?"

"Hey, George, I couldn't help but overhear what ya said, so how about dropping me off up near Ninth Street. You're going right past there, you know, if you're takin' Curt and Dan up to Hill Street."

"Yeah, man, I can dig what you're sayin', but if you heard what I said, you must not have heard the part I said about I ain't no fuckin' taxi, you dig? I'm doing Curtis a favor 'cause I want him to do somethin' for me, but I ain't got no time to drop you off on Ninth Street, Hip Daddy," George stated, then hit the button and ran his window back up before the man could say anything else.

George spoke to the two men inside the car. "I can't get *over the nerve of some of these niggers*. I mean, look at that shit Hip Daddy is wearing. Them pants he got on are filthy. Now common sense should tell him that I don't want him in my ride with all that grease on his clothes. Shit, I'd never get it out of this white upholstery I got. But if I was to tell him the truth, his feelings would be hurt, while I'd be in trouble if I was stupid enough to let him in my ride."

Curtis had to agree with him. One look at the nasty overhalls that Hip Daddy wore was enough to make George's point. The man looked as if he had been working on some cars in a garage somewhere. Dirt and oil was everywhere on the man's pants. But it hadn't stopped him from asking for a ride. In fact, Curtis reflected as he thought about it, he doubted if the thought had even entered Hip Daddy's mind.

"Now what can I do for you guys?" George inquired, as he drove away from the curb.

Curtis waited until he had turned a corner before asking, "You know what I asked you about last week, don't you, George?"

"Yeah, I just forget how much it was. I can handle it, you dig, that ain't no problem. Now what was it you wanted? Was it raw stuff, or mixed dope. Which one, it don't make no difference to me which one you want."

"We got a bill fifty," Dan said quickly, causing Curtis to flinch angrily.

George let out a short laugh. "Hey amigo, don't worry about it, old George ain't goin' give you no screwing. You ain't got to worry. Now let's get down to facts. You guys are just gettin' started, right?"

He waited until Curtis had nodded his head in agreement, then continued, "Okay then, dig this. Curt, you ain't got no milk sugar yet have you?" Again he waited for the head shake, "Okay, then, now listen while I pull your coat to something. If you ain't got the right bankroll, it's goin' set you

by Al C. Clark

back tryin' to buy milk sugar to cut your dope with." George hesitated briefly, letting his words sink in. "Now I don't give a shit what you buy, Curt, but since you're just gettin' started, I can help you out."

"Okay, George, I know we don't know that much about this jive, but we ain't above listenin' to somebody who can pull our coats to the real deal."

George let out a short laugh. "Okay, good, we got a understandin', that's good. I like you Curt, that ain't no bullshit. If I didn't I wouldn't waste my time. Now, dig this. It would be better if you bought mixed dope from me this time. While you're selling it, you can use some of the money you make and purchase the milk sugar you'll be needin' when your money is right and you buy raw dope."

"How much is the mix goin' cost us?" Dan inquired seriously.

"Too much!" George replied quickly. "Unless you're got more than one fifty. If that's all the cash you've got, you're going to need it to get started. Or," he continued with a large smile, "you had better go and find another Fernandez brother and bust him."

"Well I'll be damn," Dan cursed quietly. "It don't take long for shit to spread, does it?"

"Aw hell, Dan," Curt said, "don't you know Mexicans are tight as hell? Don't nothing happen to one that the rest of them don't find out about."

Again George let out his phony laugh. "That's right, especially when one gets played on by one of you brothers, the message spreads quickly."

"Played on hell, the bastard just lost his money, that's all," Dan alibied quickly.

"Yeah, man," George replied, drawing the last word out, "I know just what you mean."

"Fuck that shit!" Curtis stated sharply. "It ain't no skin off your ass no way, is it George?"

George shook his head quickly. "Naw," he answered, the lie revealed in every line in his face. "Why the shit should I care what some dumb ass spic goes and does. As long as it wasn't my money, I could care less."

Both the Black men knew at once that the man was lying to them. Curtis asked what was on both of their minds. "I hope that shit don't cause us to fall out over the dope you sell me George. I mean, I dig you and all that shit, but my money comes too damn hard for me to get some bunk for it."

"Hey, amigo, this is George you're talkin' to. Like I said, whatever some other cat goes and does don't mean shit to me, and if it did, I wouldn't let it come before me and my business, Curtis."

Curtis nodded his head in agreement. "I'm hoping you see it that away, George, because if we work it right, there will be plenty of green stuff in it for both of us."

"Yeah man," Dan said, speaking his little bit. "It ain't about nothin', that crap game, 'cause it was

by Al C. Clark

me that beat them dudes out of their bread anyway, not Curt."

It was obvious that George was irritated by
Dan's words. "Listen, man," he began, "me and
Curt are going to do the business, you dig? I don't
know nothing about you, so if you don't mind,
you stay out of it. I know you were the one who
rolled the dice, as well as I know that if Curtis
hadn't been there, they would have took their
money back."

The man's words stung. Dan winced under them
but before he could speak, Curtis spoke up because
he knew that Dan's pride had been hurt.

"We should completely forget about the crap
game, George, it was unavoidable, and I regret that
it happened."

"Well I don't," Dan yelled, continuing to keep
the subject open. "If the studs were out of their
league playin' that was their problem, not mine."

"Hey, man," George said softly, "the studs
thought it was just a friendly game. They didn't
know Curtis was in on the hustle. I mean, shootin'
craps in Curtis' back yard has always been a thing
we have gone in for. After today, who knows, but I
can promise you this, you won't ever pick up any
more easy money like that!"

"Shit!" Curtis cursed, "you guys just ain't going
to let it drop, are you?" He took out his cigarettes
and quickly lit one. "If you want me to, George,
I'll make the guys' money right. I just want an end

to it."

George shrugged his fat shoulders. "Forget it, man. It's over and done. Pedro needed a lesson, now maybe he'll believe he ain't the smartest guy in the world."

"You can say that again," Dan stated, then laughed sardonically.

For some reason, Dan seemed to get on George's nerves. Every time he spoke, the fat man seemed to get aroused. "You know, Curt, it don't take all of us to take care of this business, so why don't we drop your friend off somewhere and you can pick him back up when you get back over here."

"No bet, man. My money ain't going out of my sight," Dan said angrily.

"Hold it," Curtis said quickly. "You realize what you're sayin', Dan?" as his temper rose. "George, stop at the corner and let Dan out. My mother stays about five blocks from here. If you want to, you can walk over there and wait until I get back with the stuff. If not, well it's your decision."

Before Curtis was finished speaking, George had pulled to the curb and parked. Dan glared angrily at the fat man. "Hey, Curt, let me talk to you privately for a second, huh?"

"Hey, man, I ain't got all day. Either we take care of the business, or pass it up to another fuckin' time," George stated.

Curtis shook his head. "It ain't necessary for all

by Al C. Clark

that shit, Dan. I know what's got to be done, so
why go to all this bullshit." Curtis was trying to
make his partner cool down.

"Fuck that shit, Curt," Dan said hotly. "This fat
motha-fucker thinks he's playin' games with us,
but it ain't about nothing, Curt. We can cop some
jive anyplace. We ain't got to deal with this chili
bean-eatin' motherfucker!"

"Hey man, I ain't got to me all them names,"
George said slowly, his fat cheeks turning red.

"You'll be all them names and any more I want
to call you, fat ass motherfucker," Dan yelled, as
he opened the car door.

"Dan, Dan," Curtis yelled at his friend, "cool
down a minute, man. This shit ain't about nothing.
It ain't no problem for you to wait until I get back
from coppin', man."

"I ain't waitin' nowhere, Curt. We began together and we'll finish together, if we're going to
be real partners."

The two men glared at each other. Then Curtis
broke the short silence. "Well, it don't make sense
coppin' nowhere else, Dan. George got the best jive
in the city, so it ain't good business to go
elsewhere."

"The fat motherfucker don't want to do no
business with me, Curt, cause I trimmed them
other bean-eatin' motherfuckin' spics, man. So I
ain't about to kiss his ass to get along with him,"
Dan stated loudly.

41

"Ain't nobody asked you to do nothin', Dan. All you got to do is give me your bread and wait until I get back, that's all."

Dan shook his head stubbornly. "Like I said before, Curt, I ain't about to let my money get out of my sight. Now if he wants to do business with us, he'll do it with both of us, like he started out to do. Other than that, he can kiss my black ass!"

Dan slammed the car door and glared back through the open window. "It ain't nothing about you, Curt, it's just that I don't like the way this fat motherfucker came down on us. Now if you want to still go through with it yourself, that's up to you."

"Yeah, man," Curtis answered softly, "I ain't changed my mind. George still got the best dope in town, and I want some of it."

With slow deliberation, Dan spit on the hood of the car, then slowly extracted the bankroll from his pocket. His cold black eyes never left the face of the angry Mexican. He counted out the money, then pushed seventy-five dollars back through the window.

"Here's your share of the money for trimming them two trick-ass Mexicans, Curt. If you ever get some more dumb ass wetbacks over your way, give me a ring and I'll be glad to come over and relieve them stupid motherfuckers from their bankroll!" As soon as he finished speaking, he again spit on top of the car's hood, making sure George saw him do it.

George pulled away from the curb quickly, his cheeks a flaming red. He couldn't hide his anger, nor could he hide the fear that had gripped him. For a brief minute, he hadn't known which way the angry Negro would go. Violence was one thing he wanted no part of, not when he might be on the receiving end of it.

"That crazy sonofvabitch," George said as he drove swiftly through the traffic, "I'll fix his fuckin' ass one of these days, Curt, I promise you that!"

Both men fell silent, each thinking his own bitter thoughts. Curt realized that now his money wasn't nowhere near right. How could he cop with only half the price of a bag. He came right to the point.

"Well, ain't no reason for me to beat around the bush, George," he began. "You went and blew it for me. I needed Dan's share of the money to make my bankroll right. When you went out of your way to arouse him, you blew it for me!"

Fat George shrugged his shoulders, then lit a cigar. The smell of the brown cigar filled the car. "Don't worry about it, Curt. Like I said, I alway have liked you, so we can make it up whenever you cop again." He waited for a second, then added, "How does that sound to you, huh?"

For the first time since Dan got out, Curtis sat back and relaxed. Things might work out even better now. Without a partner there would be more money for him and less of a problem.

"Yeah, George," he replied, smiling briefly, "things just might work out all right after all."

3

FAT GEORGE TOOK THE TWO LANE HIGHWAY out
of Cloves and drove into the desert night. After
they had passed the small trucker's diner at the
city limits, there was no sign of life anywhere. The
smooth-riding car was engulfed in blackness and
silence.

Curtis reached down and turned on the radio,
letting the mellow sounds of Coltrain flow through
the car. He slouched down in his seat, feeling
better about his situation than he had for some
time.

"You look mighty mellow, my man," George
said after a while.

"Yeah. I dig the scene that's coming down. I've

been trying to get it together for a long time, George."

George reached into his pocket and pulled out a pack of fresh cigarettes. He offered one to Curtis, then took one for himself. After lighting both, he spoke. "I could see that, amigo. I been watching you myself . . . you know, keeping the antennae out there for a dude like yourself who might be makin' his move."

Curtis looked at George and noticed the fat man smiling. His lips were pulled back, with the cigarette dangling from the corner of his mouth. "You dig this scene?" Curtis asked.

"Sometimes, my man, it's shit. And then, sometimes it's mellow. I like to keep it soft and cool, if you know what I mean. Then, when the bread comes, the woman has some nice threads, and the junkies stay popped."

"Yeah" Curtis replied, exhaling the smoke from his cigarette, "I dig where you're coming from."

The two men, one Black and one Mexican, drove through the desert night. Curtis did not ask where George was taking him, that wasn't the kind of question a dude like himself out on his first score asked a heavy-weight like George. All Curtis knew, and cared to know for the moment, was that the fat man was leading him down the trail of white powder, towards that score that would set him up.

The better part of an hour had drifted by when Curtis saw the lights of a small town in the distance. He read the sign as they passed. The town of Las Vegas was ten miles ahead; Las Vegas, New Mexico, where men gambled their souls and not their money.

"What's this shit, George?" Curtis yelled after realizing what their destination was.

"What's what shit, Curtis?"

"Las Vegas, man! Shit, the fuckin' town's never seen nothin' but the brown powder from Mexico. I'm tryin' to cop the white shit, and you take me to the home of the brown stuff. Shit, Man!!!"

George was laughing at Curtis. His body shook, the fat rolling around his neck and cheeks like small waves. "Hey man, let me pull your coat to something . . . if you just control yourself long enough to listen."

Curtis was fuming. For the moment, anyway, he had thought that George was setting him up. Not that the man wasn't going to score him some smack, but that he was going to score him the brown stuff. It was a bad scene for a dealer to get stuck with too much of that Mexican stuff because any junkie in his right mind could make the hour's drive into Las Vegas and settle his own accounts, without using the dealer as a middle man.

It was, always has been and always will be the white stuff that brings the dudes crawling—no matter where a man might decide to go into business.

"You listening, baby? Or you goin' to think that maybe I'm some kind of funky dude who's out for a half-set?"

"Okay, George. You better lay it on me like it is . . . " Curtis stared straight ahead, not wanting to meet George's glance from the other end of the seat.

"All right, my man. That's better. Now you know I run the stuff in Cloves, right?"

"Right" Curtis said, now anxious for George to get to the point.

"But Cloves don't have its mainline, does it? I mean, on one trucks the stuff in there all the time. So a man like myself who wants to keep his people happy and mellow twenty-fours a day has to get his stuff from somewhere. Las Vegas is the place, man. It's the mainline for this whole fuckin' part of the country."

Curtis knew that George was right. But what George had told him so far was not news. Everyone living in the Southwestern desert who had a habit, or desired to make a little extra income off other loser's habits, knew about Las Vegas. It was one of those towns that somehow came into its own, passing illegal contraband between Mexico and the United States.

First, it was grass, then a little mescaline, some cocaine and finally the heavy stuff. The police knew about it, but they didn't seem to take their jobs too seriously, because the town flourished as more and more junk came through.

"But it's all brown shit, man!" Curtis said.

by Al C. Clark

"Everyone else's is brown, my man, except for your man's here. For some reason the law doesn't mess with the brown shit . . . but the white stuff gets to them. I got my main man stationed right here, mixed in with the brown passers. It's a beautiful little happening, Curtis."

George was pleased with himself. A smile of great satisfaction etched its way across his face.

Curtis held his breath as they drove onto the main street of the small college town. The road was lined with little chicken joints and hamburger stands. Black, brown and white dudes slouched easily against the buildings watching the big Cadillac cruise by. It occurred to Curtis at that moment that possibly George was fixing to set him up with his main man here in Las Vegas. Possibly George wanted him in the business, right now and without further delay.

As much as the idea would have pleased Curtis, though, he knew the odds were stacked against that ever happening. A man doesn't deal smack because he wants to donate his coin to charity. A man deals because he discovers it's easier to live off of people's weakness than to work for a living. But the road isn't easy, and a man like George wasn't about to hand over his gains to some nigger beginner like Curtis. No, Curtis thought, the man simply wants to show me why I should keep dealing with him. Nothing more, nothing less.

"You see, my man" George said as he turned

into the parking lot of a Denny's restaurant, "it's tough to get the good stuff. Ain't no way a man can pull white powder out of brown."

George looked across the seat at Curtis and winked. Curtis knew his guess was right. The man was making a point, showing him that his connection was solid—solid enough so that he could even take Curtis this far.

"Okay, George" Curtis began, opening the door, "I dig where you're coming from I'll cop from you as long as the stuff remains solid."

"And you'll get rich doing it, my man. Very, very rich."

Curtis stepped out of the car, walked around to George's window and leaned in. "How long?"

"Give me about twenty minutes, Curt. This dude is very heavy and likes to work slow. He's as solid as you can get, though, so there's no hassle."

George rolled the electric window up and drove out of the parking lot. Curtis watched the taillights of the Cadillac until they disappeared around a corner a block down the main street. He turned and walked into the garishly lit restaurant.

Curtis ordered a glass of milk and a piece of apple pie. He drummed his fingers nervously on the counter top as he waited for the little blonde waitress to bring him his food. He watched the girl, she couldn't have been no more than eighteen, as she reached up above her head for the pie. The little white dress she wore rode up the back of her thighs. She was built nicely there, with a small ass and rich, muscular thighs. For a fraction of a second, Curtis caught the line running between those thighs. The chick was wearing pantyhose, but no panties.

"You're new here, aren't you?" the chick asked, setting the food down in front of Curtis.

"Naw, baby. I just never graced this joint before, that's all." Curtis knew it was a good idea to never tell the truth, especially to a white chick.

"Oh. You attend the college?" Her name was Linda Sue. That was spelled out conveniently on the small white tag that rested just above her tit.

"Thinkin' about it, honey. Not sure yet if there's anything there for me, though." Curtis was enjoying the little game. He had sized her up the minute she had opened her mouth. A white bitch, probably from the south. Her parents had probably spent the better part of her childhood telling her horrible and awful tales of the "nigras" and their sexual prowess and passion. "Why, them people jus' go 'round fuckin' like rabbits . . . an' ya'll know what they say 'bout them Nigra men!" Curtis almost broke out laughing thinking about it.

Linda Sue's big blue eyes were set upon Curtis, and she smiled, showing even, white teeth. Curtis thought about it but knew it wouldn't be cool to get mixed up with some white chick, especially on this night.

"I work here every night. Come on in around

closing time some night and I'll show you the sights." Linda Sue was not that taken that she did not forget to write out his bill.

"What I've seen so far, baby, seems mighty fine to me . . ." Curtis drank his milk slowly, resting his eyes on her full tits.

"They get better. Much better." She had made her point, there was nothing left to say. Linda Sue looked up from her order pad, ripped off the bill, and tried to place the paper on the counter in a seductive manner. But she misjudged and put the check directly on top of Curtis' apple pie.

"Hey baby, if I wanted some topping, you know I would have asked for it!"

Curtis watched her fumble with the check, then slam it down angrily next to his plate. She turned away from him and walked quickly down the length of the counter. He knew he had blown her out. It was so easy sometimes that it made him laugh.

A strong, chilly wind began to rip across the desert, blowing sand and dust in swirls around the Denny's parking lot. Curtis stood sheltered against the restroom wall, waiting for the man who would bring him the start of his business.

One cigarette later, George pulled into the lot, drove up next to Curtis and leaned across the seat to open the door for him. He was grinning broadly.

"Hey my man, what it is?" Curtis said, pulling the door shut behind him.

"Everything, just everything is groovy . . ." George was mellow, grinning from ear to ear. He pulled out of the parking lot and headed back down the road towards Cloves. The winds were blowing hard on the open highway, but the big, heavy Cadillac bucked them nicely.

"Here, Curtis. A little something to keep you warm." George handed Curtis a brown paper bag. Curtis opened the sack and pulled out a plastic bag that contained the purest, whitest smack he had ever seen.

"Oh yeah, baby! I can dig it! Beautiful!!!" Curtis rolled the bag around and around in his hands.

"Cut that stuff about five to one, amigo, and you'll be doing the junkies a favor!"

But Curtis had other plans. Five to one was the norm, everyone who dealt cut it that way. To start his business off on the right foot, give his customers something to come back to, Curtis had decided a long time ago that he would bomb them with a four to one cut. It would be the best deal in town. And besides, he knew he could pull it off because of one important fact. Curtis did not use the stuff himself. At no time would there be a desire to rip some off for his own pleasure, and there wouldn't be the temptation to cut it down so that he could shoot himself. No, Curtis thought to himself, this is one fuckin' dude who's goin' to play the game with a little class!

"Well?" George was driving with both hands on the wheel, bucking the strong winds. He smiled over at Curtis.

"It's good, my man. I believe that the black and the brown are goin' to do some nice jive together."

"How 'bout snortin' a little of the magic powder, Curtis?" George was still grinning at him.

Curtis turned down to the bag in his hands. A strange feeling overcame him. He couldn't explain it, but he had the definite sensation that George was up to something.

"Aw, come on, Curtis." There was a tone of daring in George's voice. "It ain't nothin' 'bout nothin'. You know what I mean?"

"Well," Curtis began slowly, placing the small packet into his pocket, "not this time, George. You know I don't use."

"Sometimes it ain't bad to relax a little. Especially after a big night like tonight." George reached under the seat of the car and pulled out a bottle of Johnnie Walker Red. He passed it to Curtis.

"Thanks, George. I sure can use some of this . . ."

As Curtis took a large sip from the bottle, he had the strange feeling that George was disappointed about something. But once the mellow juice soothed his nerves, Curtis forgot about it. There wasn't anything that was going to ruin the good feeling he had. Cruising through the desert in

by Al C. Clark

a smooth Caddie, a full bottle of Johnnie Walker Red and a long, empty highway ahead of them was enough. The weight of the small packet of white powder in his pocket only added to the groove.

4

IT TOOK ONLY A COUPLE OF WEEKS for the man
with the four-to-one pop to gain a reputation. The
junkies down on Main Street began dropping by
Curtis' pad day and night, seeking the fine white
powder that mixed a little more to their liking than
the other stuff in town.

Curtis was making the bread, and Fat George
couldn't have been more pleased with the arrange-
ment. He was supplying Curtis, giving him any
quantity that he needed, leaving himself open for
more leisure time and a little less hassle. The one
goal that George sought was to get himself away
from the addicts, far enough away so that their
unpredictable behavior would never affect him.
Pushing his stuff through Curtis was the man's way
of handling it.

by Al C. Clark

For both men, the situation seemed to have a future. They could each look ahead, count their money, and plan on making gains.

After two months of hustling the streets, Curtis decided it was time to settle into a more reputable scene. His lifestyle was suspect, he knew that he could be spotted easily, and that his movements left little doubt as to what he did for a living. With the amount of money he was making, and the kinds of dudes he was selling to, he decided that it was high time to get himself into a cozy little apartment—at least for the time being.

It was a hot, muggy afternoon. Curtis cruised around in his old Buick for three hours, following up ads for apartments that he had seen in the local newspaper. He knew what he was looking for, but none of the places he had seen so far fit the bill.

Curtis wanted a place where there were lots of people; kids and their mothers, fathers coming home from work, and a couple of times a week bringing a few of the boys with them for beer. He wanted action around him, bodies moving all the time. That kind of a place would make his comings and goings, plus the ceaseless flow of junkies that would be visiting him, much less obvious. Alone in a secluded little place would raise the suspicion of the nosy neighbors who tended to live in those kinds of places. For the time being, anyway, Curtis wanted to lose himself in a crowd.

The end of the day was approaching fast, and

Curtis knew he didn't have much time left. He had people coming at eight o'clock that night, meeting him in the back yard of his mother's place. The sun was low in the western sky, and the mugginess of the day had all but worn him out.

There was one last apartment house on his list, a place located just three blocks off of Main Street. Curtis figured that the location was good, because most of the junkies he dealt with didn't have rides, and a place within walking distance would pick his business up. He drove over to the Paradise Apartments and stopped in front.

The building was old and gray, with two dilapidated palm trees in front. Curtis leaned out his window and peered through the iron gates into the courtyard. A small pool was filled with children, and he could see three or four motherly types sitting around, smoking cigarettes and talking. The scene looked right.

The manager was an old, Black woman with two teeth missing in front. She talked with a lisp, and shook the stairway when she led Curtis up to the second floor apartment.

"A young dude like yourself . . . this is a good place." She smiled obscenely up at him, holding the door open.

The apartment was a one bedroom, furnished in deep green, and generally clean. The kitchen window looked out onto the street, and Curtis thought that a good point. Anybody coming toward the building from Main Street would have to make the turn at that end of the street. They would be visible from his kitchen.

"How much, ma'am?" Curtis asked, giving the lady his best college grin.

"Hunnerd an' ten. . . ."

Curtis reached into his pocket, aware of the lady's careful watch. He pulled out three hundred dollar bills, and a fifty.

"Here," he said, handing her the three-fifty, "take it for the next three months. I don't want to be hassled with no rent for that amount of time. You dig?"

"Yessir!" the old woman replied, holding the money and wavering back and forth between giving him change or trying to rip him off for the extra twenty.

Curtis showed her to the front door, took the doorkey from her, and led her out onto the balcony. "And listen, ma'am, you just take that extra twenty in there and buy yourself something nice. Okay?"

The old woman was speechless. She looked up at Curtis and smiled, clutching the money in her hands. As Curtis watched her walk unsteadily across the balcony toward the stairway, he knew that there would be no problem from her—ever.

From that moment on, Curtis began working out of his new pad. It was easy going. The junkies liked it there and felt safe. The people who lived around him never knew what was coming down. They were all too busy with their own lives to worry about the lean, dark dude who had moved in upstairs. It was a good scene, and was to get even better.

Curtis saw Shirley the second day. He was standing out on the balcony, having just made a good three hundred off of one dude who was about to take a little journey to L.A. and needed some warmth for his ride on the bus. Curtis was feeling good, sipping a beer and watching the women and their children down by the pool.

Shirley was sitting with her three children on the patio. She was light-skinned, Mexican, with a head of the finest, blackest hair he had ever seen. Most of the other women around the pool were fat, and showed the signs of too many children. But not Shirley. Her bikini was small enough to reveal her long, lean legs and her rich, full thighs. Her stomach was flat, and her breasts pushed evenly against her tiny bra. Curtis watched her for the better part of an hour as she languished beneath the hot New Mexican sun.

Curtis' attention was diverted by a tall, black dude who ambled into the courtyard. He watched as the man walked across the patio below and walked directly toward Shirley. The beautiful woman said something to one of the other ladies, then got up and walked back toward her first floor apartment. The black dude followed her, making his way along the opposite side of the pool. Curtis watched as he disappeared into her apartment.

He had never spoken with the girl, but Curtis was fuming. He couldn't understand the anger he felt, or the disappointment. It seemed impossible that he would even have a chance with such a beautiful woman, but nevertheless, the rage was still there.

When the man appeared after only a couple of minutes, Curtis was relieved. At least the chick wasn't a working whore. He had seen so many housewives take on afternoon jobs to keep the spending money coming in that he automatically assumed that that was what this woman was doing. But two minutes wasn't even long enough time for them to get mellow.

The black man walked across the patio and left the apartment building. Shirley came out of her apartment a moment later. While she walked back toward her kids, she looked up at Curtis and smiled. It was the kind of look that made Curtis uncomfortable, because it revealed a knowledge in her.

The next day, Curtis watched from his living room window. He saw his old friend and onetime partner, Dan, walk into the courtyard and go to Shirley's apartment. Dan emerged a second later, strutting happily back toward the entrance.

"Dan, my man. What it is?" Curtis shouted down.

Dan stopped in his tracks, looked up at the figure of Curtis. "Hey! Curtis, baby. Wha's happenin'?"

"Come on up, Dan. Show you my pad. . . . I just moved in here!"

Dan looked around for a moment. He was always suspicious. When he had decided that there was nothing going on, he climbed the steps to the second story, ambled up to Curtis and gave him a slap.

"Long time, man," Dan said, smiling.

"Yeah, baby. Come on inside and have a beer. I got some things I got to know."

Dan looked at his old friend curiously, then followed Curtis into the apartment. There was still the tension of that night with Fat George between them, and Dan was highly aware of his own feelings. He was also badly in need of a fix. But that would have to wait, because Dan wasn't about to admit to Curtis that he was mainlining. A few snorts had been his scene when they had been together ripping the Fernandez brothers off for a few nickels and dimes. But that had been the limit. Curtis was one of those dudes you didn't admit to using in front of, because Curtis didn't use himself. And Dan knew that Curtis would never consider taking him on as a partner if he found out that Dan was on the needle.

Dan still had hopes of getting in on the scoring end; but at the same time he knew that his chances for making it in that kind of scene were evaporating as fast as he could puncture his veins with the needle. Time was definitely not on his side, it hadn't been since the night he had confronted Fat George.

Curtis came out of the kitchen with two cans of beer. He tossed one to Dan, then sat down in the armchair, resting his feet on the coffee table.

"How you been, Dan?"

"Groovy, Curtis. Nothin' happenin' with me that ain't fine. . . ." Dan took a long swig of his beer.

"Still snortin' the powder?"

Dan lowered his can and stared down at the floor. "Ain't nothin' about nothin' doin' that shit, Curtis. You know that as well as me."

"Yeah," Curtis replied, "but that chick down there don't." Curtis was taking a chance, hoping that his guess about the beautiful woman was correct. From the look on Dan's face, he knew that he had batted a thousand.

"Yeah, well. Just a little of the snortin' stuff, you know what I mean. She's cool about short change . . . I mean, really cool."

"I dig where you're comin' from, Dan. She looks like a together momma."

Dan grinned, then drank some more of his beer. He cleared his throat and set the can down on the table top. Leaning forward, he began to speak. "Listen, Curtis, I'll be more than happy to set you up with Shirley. She's fine, and doesn't mess with no one, if you dig what I mean."

Curtis started to tell Dan that it wouldn't be necessary, but Dan waved him off.

"No man, nothin' about nothin'. That's all right. But one thing . . ." Dan leaned a little closer. There was a special look in his eyes as he spoke. "I hear stuff about you, man. I'm not surprised, you know what I mean, but I hear the thing. You an' me started like brothers, man, and then that fat Mexican screwed us up. Why not pick it up, you know, make it a partnership again."

His words were soft and uncertain. Curtis felt sorry for his old friend. But he knew how unstable Dan was, and how easy it was for him to screw things up.

"Listen Dan," Curtis began, "let me pull your coat to something. Right now, I've got to move alone. By myself without no one else around, you dig? I mean, this is some motherfuckin' loose town, but not that loose. I hope I've made myself clear on that point."

Dan pushed his beer can aside and stood up. Curtis could see that he was trembling. For a moment, Curtis felt himself tighten to the possibility of a fight. But after looking at Dan closer, he saw that the man was in no condition.

"Easy, baby. Ain't nothin' personal or anythin' like that. . . ."

"You motherfucker!" Dan screamed. "You bastard! You and that cocksuckin' Mexican bean-eater done fucked me up! I was all set, ready to make it with our plan, and you went with that mother-fucker instead! Goddamn, man!"

"You listen, Dan," Curtis said, standing up, "you're the fuckin' fool who fucked it up! Man, we had it made and you went and blew the whole damn thing!"

Dan knew that Curtis was right. Besides, Curtis was one dude who Dan could never argue with. He had never won anything from Curtis. His only victories came off the Fernandez brothers.

"All right, man," Dan said in a much softer voice, "I dig where you're coming from."

Dan stopped at the front door before leaving. "I got to take care of some business, Curtis. You be cool. . . ." He slammed the door behind him.

Curtis watched him leave through the kitchen window. The man didn't even have a ride. He walked all the way down the block then turned the corner toward Main Street. Curtis didn't like the way the dude was turning out. There was some-thing loose inside him that made him worry. He decided, though, that it wouldn't pay off to sit around and worry, because there were a thousand dudes like Dan. It was just unfortunate that he happened to have had some earlier business deal-ings with him.

The afternoon was turning into evening. Curtis watched Shirley's apartment, then finally decided to make his move. He put on his best shirt, his leather pants and his suede boots.

She opened the door wearing a terrycloth robe that was partially open. Curtis looked at the smooth brown skin between the bulge of her breasts. She smiled at him, showing even, white teeth. "I've been expecting you, Curtis," she said, opening the door wider.

At that moment, Curtis knew that he had it made. He and Shirley got pretty thick pretty quick!

5

AS HE LOOKED AROUND THE APARTMENT taking in the new furniture, Curt's chest swelled with pride. His woman, Shirley, was in the kitchen preparing a quick lunch for him and her three children. He stretched his legs on the gold-colored couch and patted the cushion. The smell of the new furniture filled his nostrils as he inhaled deeply. Give me another month, he reflected, and he just might have a new house. At the rate the dope was selling, it shouldn't take too much longer. First thing, though, he was going to get him a new car. The old 1955 Buick he had bought was good for now, but for a man as fast as he was, it just wasn't his speed. What he really wanted was a new Cadillac. That was more down his line than some antique Buick.

"Honey," Shirley called from the kitchen, "do you want rye bread or white with your ham?"

"Put mine on white bread," Curt answered, as he got up and moved the marble-topped coffee table out of the way. Curtis removed a small package from his pocket and shook out the white powder onto an album cover. He then took his driver's license and packed the white powder into a smooth pile in front of him. He took an old strainer that his woman used in the kitchen and ran the dope through it. After he was sure it was good and strained, he shook out some more white powder from another package. He quickly mixed the two powders together. By the time he had it mixed, his woman came out of the kitchen carrying his sandwich.

"I hope you finish with that stuff before the children come home from school for their lunch break," Shirley said.

He glanced up at the attractive, light-skinned woman. She was wearing a pair of black hotpants that did more than just reveal her lovely shape. Her well-shaped long legs seemed to be flawless. As she set the dish containing the food down in front of him, he ran his hand slowly down her lovely legs.

"Goddamn," Curtis said, as he pulled her down onto his lap and kissed her passionately. He ran his hands through her long black hair. As he played with a string of it, he kissed her on the ear. You are one lucky motherfucker, Curtis, he said to himself as she returned his kiss.

Shirley slowly pushed him away. "Honey," she began, "I wish you would take care of your business in such a way so that that fat bastard George wouldn't have to come here." She hesitated, then added, "at least whenever you're not here. I don't like for him to come in when you're not here."

Curtis raised up and stared into her eyes. "Shirley, don't give me no shit, now. What did he do, or try to do to you, while I wasn't here?"

She shook her head. "He didn't try and do nothing, Curt. It's just the things he hints at. You know what I mean."

"The hell I do," he said half angrily. "I don't have the slightest idea of what he says, so pull my coat!"

Again she hesitated, then said, "Well, you know. Me being part Mexican and all that shit. He hints around it, you know, why don't I have a Chicago, or did I ever have a Mexican boyfriend. Shit like that. Nothing out of the way, you know, that you could get mad at, but I just don't like him. The way he looks at me, and all that shit!"

Curtis grinned at her. "Well, I can't really blame him for lookin' at you, Shirley. You know, you're one hell of an eyeful for anybody, and I'm one happy motherfucker to have you for my woman!"

She smiled and bent over and kissed him. "You better finish packaging that stuff up, the kids will be here for lunch in another five minutes." She climbed off his lap. "We won't get anything done with me sittin' here on top of you."

"Oh baby, we'll get something done, all right, it just might not be what·you had on your mind, that's all."

They laughed together, then she blew him a kiss from a safe distance. "Okay, lover man. You finish what you're doing, and I'll think of some way to thank you for the lovely furniture. It's just too beautiful for words."

"If you can't think of anything, I might have an idea of how you can repay me," Curtis said, and leered at her in such a way that she knew just what he was talking about.

"Oh my God," she replied, mockingly, "I've got a sex fiend on my hands!"

Curtis waited until she disappeared back into the kitchen before he began to pack the dope into balloons. First he would put an empty balloon on the end of a small funnel, then he'd put a small spoon of dope into a measuring spoon, then empty it into the funnel and shake it down until it went into the small balloon. After that, he'd roll up the balloon into a small bundle and tie small knots into the end of it.

Curtis had just finished with the last balloon and was counting them when the doorbell rang. Shirley came out of the kitchen and went to the door. She cast a quick glance in his direction to make sure all of the dope was out of sight before opening the door.

As he stuffed the balloons in his coat pocket, Curtis counted them slowly. Twenty-five balloons at twenty dollars apiece. It wasn't too bad, but it wasn't too much of an Earthshaker either, he reflected, taking his hand out of his pocket as the first child came rushing through the door.

"Hi, Daddy," the little six-year-old girl yelled as she came past. She was a small replica of her mother—the same long black hair with the flashing dark eyes. Following close behind her was her little brother. At four years of age, he resembled his mother and sister, yet had the height of the man who had sired him. He was already taller than his older sister, but that was the only difference between them in appearance. He looked as much like her as it was possible for a boy to favor a girl without being funny. Behind him came his double, only his twin brother didn't quite have the height that he had. They were almost impossible to tell apart.

Both of the boys called Curtis Daddy as they went by, but they used the word in name only. There was nothing about Curtis in any of the children. Either one of the three could have passed for a Mexican whenever they wanted too. There were no distinctive Negro characteristics about any of the children.

After the children filed past into the kitchen, Curtis ate his food slowly, enjoying every bit as he studied the living room of the apartment. What he needed, he decided, was some matching wall to wall carpet on the floor, something that would bring out the expensive furniture he had just bought. The drapes were a light brown, so they matched the rest of the stuff in the apartment fairly well, but he wasn't satisfied with what he saw. He knew it would take time.

Curtis was suddenly interrupted from his daydreams by the doorbell. Shirley came out of the kitchen and went to the door. She peeped out of the peephole, then took off the night chain. She opened the door and stepped back.

As Dan walked into the apartment, Curtis was surprised to see how skinny the man looked as compared to the last time he had seen him. He knew now that Dan was using stuff, but it was no surprise. He had known before that Dan liked to snort heroin, but from what he had heard, Dan was now a mainliner.

"What it is, Curt," Dan called out as he stepped into the apartment. "Long time no see." Dan held out his hand.

Curtis slapped it in a friendly manner, then sat back down. "Yeah, bro, it's been a while since I last saw you, but I been hearing about you here and there."

"Yeah, Curt, I'll just bet you have," Dan said, then continued. "Say my man, you got some of that good stuff, ain't you?"

by Al C. Clark

Curtis shook his head. "Yeah, bro, I got a few bags. What was it you wanted to cop, Dan?" Curtis asked, after taking a quick glance at the kitchen to make sure none of the kids were in hearing distance.

A sly look came into Dan's yellowish eyes as he stared at his old buddy. "You ain't got nothing but them twenties made up, have you Curt?" he inquired sharply.

Curtis nodded his head in agreement. "Yeah, man, if you want something bigger than that, I can't help you. If you'll let me know ahead of time, I can get it for you though."

"Naw, naw, baby, I don't want no big thing. All I want is a twenty-dollar bag, but the problem is, Curt, I ain't got but ten dollars."

Curtis glanced up at the man. "Dan, don't play games with me, now. You wouldn't have come by here to cop with your money that short, 'cause you know Shirley couldn't let you go for that amount."

Dan held up his hand. "Hey, Bro, I never would have stopped if I hadn't seen your old ride sittin' outside. Since I knew you were here, I decided to come up and give it a try for old times sake, you know what I mean?"

For a brief second, Curtis was going to turn him down, then changed his mind. "Okay, Dan, this time I'll go along with it, but don't come to me that short again, hear?"

"Yeah, partner," Dan said with a sly smile, "you ain't got to worry about it. I don't be short that often, do I Shirley?" Dan glanced down at the rug.

She agreed with him. "Most of the time his money is right, Curt, except for a quarter or two at times."

"Okay," Curt answered as he removed a balloon from his pocket and tossed it to Dan. "Be cool when you leave out of here, Dan," he said in way of good-bye. Curtis waited until Shirley had let him back out the door, then he shook his head.

"It's hard to believe the way that man has come down in the last month," he stated.

"Shit!" Shirley exclaimed, "it ain't so hard if you understand what happened to him. You didn't want to believe it when I ran it down to you, but like I said, Fat George was behind it. He put Rose up to it. Dan thought he was coppin' a fast Mexican whore, and he wasn't doing nothing but falling into a trap George set for him. Now I don't know why George went to all the trouble to Set Dan up that way, but I swear to you it's true. I talked to Rose, and she told me about it. George paid her to play along with Dan, then make sure and put him on the needle. After that, she could leave whenever she felt like it. He took care of her habit as long as she was with Dan, and for a while kept both of them in dope."

Curtis shook his head. "It's hard to believe. I don't think George is that goddamn dangerous, but

if he did what you said he is a dirty motherfucker.
I'd hate to have him against me."

Shirley watched her man closely. "If I were you,
Curt, I wouldn't trust George as far as you do. I
don't think he likes any Black men, you included."

Curtis laughed loudly. "Shit, Shirley, that's just
about all the people he does business with. If he
didn't like Blacks, do you think he could spend all
the time he does with them?"

"Yes," she answered honestly, "I certainly do.
Especially when you stop and think about what
kind of business he is doing. Haven't you noticed
how much he enjoys toying with the addicts he
comes in touch with? And if you stop and think
about it, Curt, just think about all the times he has
tried to get you to take a snort of that junk. I can
count over ten times that I've heard him offer it to
you. 'Here Curt,' " she mocked Fat George,
" 'come on and have a littl' snort. It ain't about
nothing.' " Shirley laughed coldly. "If you think
he's your friend, Curtis, you are one dumb ass
nigger, and I mean that from the bottom of my
heart!"

Curtis glanced at her coldly. Nigger was a word
she seldom used, for any reason. But what she said
made sense, now that she had brought it to his
attention. George did go out of his way to try and
get Curtis to take a snort, even to the point of
offering him cocaine, something else he didn't
bother with. From now on, he promised himself,

he'd stay on his guard whenever he was around Fat George. The man *was* dangerous, there was no doubt about it, especially now that he knew what trouble George had gone through to make sure that he fixed Dan's wagon. George had sworn that he would, and it looked as if he had. Making a drug addict out of any man was payback enough.

"A penny for your thoughts," Shirley said sweetly as she leaned over and kissed him on the neck. Before they could get involved in anything, the kitchen door opened and the three children came out. They had washed their hands in the kitchen so they were ready to go back to school. Each child stopped and kissed Curtis on the cheek, then stopped and kissed their mother before hurrying toward the front door. Every day they rushed through their meal so that they could get back to the school grounds and play a while before the school bell rang.

Shirley watched them leave as she held the door open for them. There was a gleam in her eyes sparkling brightly as she closed the door behind them.

Curtis stood up and held his arms open for her. "If the telephone rings, or doorbell, won't anybody answer on this end," he stated as he took her into his arms. She almost ran to him. Their embrace was tender, they kissed slowly, then slipped to the floor.

As she stretched out on the rug beside him,

Curtis opened her white blouse slowly, loosening each button with care. When he had it all the way open, he began to feel for the small hook at the back that held her bra in place. At first he had trouble getting it open, then he found the catch and it came loose in his nimble fingers. Her large, well-shaped breasts were exposed and he played with one, then the other, slowly kissing each one until the nipples became hard under his manipulations. Shirley groaned, then let out a deep moan of sexual excitement. Her breath became ragged as she tried to hold back her desires.

With slow deliberation, Curtis began to kiss her longer and harder. He ran his tongue around inside her mouth, enjoying the touch of his tongue on each part of her body. Wherever he kissed her, she became aroused. Her deep moans worked to arouse him deeply.

Taking his time, Curtis began to work her hot-pants down from her hips. With them, he removed her mini panties. He pushed the silk down over her knees, then stopped and kissed the area they had just departed from. His kisses now aroused in her a hunger that wouldn't be still. Her tongue was everywhere, wherever she could reach. He could feel her warm wetness.

He finally managed to push the hotpants completely off and now she lay under him as naked as she was when she came into the world. He could feel his dick throbbing. It was hard as a rock.

Where it rested on her leg, Shirley could feel his heat and knew it was time to take him inside of her. She squirmed into position under him, and reached down and grasped the hard meat. She held it firmly, then opened her legs and guided it into her warm cunt. Instantly, she let out a brief scream, then reached up and clutched him tightly to her, drawing her legs up around his waist.

Curtis buried his face into her neck as he began to move slowly and gently into the warmness that so eagerly awaited him.

6

NARCOTICS AGENT WILLIAM BENSON, a highly paid drug addict who worked as an undercover informer, sat in the parked car moodily awaiting his new Mexico working partner. After fishing for a month, he believed he had a drug addict who would set up one of the Mexicans. The Mexican was believed to have a direct connection from across the border. What Benson regretted was the inevitable loss of a damn good connection that he was really enjoying. The dope was always good.

Benson's partner, a young Chicano who was not known in Cloves, New Mexico, approached the car. He looked like a drug addict, but was not. He was a square agent, yet of the school where he would snort drugs if it was necessary. That was the reason why the two worked so well in the border cities.

It had been a hot, summer night in August when Benson had first met his present partner, Tony Gonzia. The temperature that night had not dropped below ninety degrees. The town of Las Vegas, New Mexico had been searing. The people of the small drug town stood on the streets, unable to confront the heat inside their small rooms and houses. William Benson was just one of the many Black men standing around "Uncle Walter's Chicken Coop" that night.

"Let me lay it on you again, amigo," the short Mexican had whispered into Benson's ear, "the man is waiting there now. No sweat, you know what I mean?"

Benson looked out across the street. There were a group of junkies lounging by the hamburger joint, smoking cigarettes and talking amongst themselves in hushed voices. Benson was new in Las Vegas, and didn't know the contacts. He was trying out Pancho, the little Mexican, and felt wary about it. But he needed a fix, and he knew he was going to have to take a chance.

"All right, my man," Benson said finally, "take me to the place. This heat is doing me in. . . ."

Pancho grinned at him with a toothless smile. "You're on, baby. . . ."

Pancho led Benson down the main street, then to a small alleyway, through a vacant lot and to the rear door of a large warehouse. There was a bright light outside the door, and when Pancho reached it he unscrewed the naked bulb. Both men waited in darkness until a maroon Cadillac turned into the alleyway and stopped next to the rear entrance.

"There it is, my man. Be cool." And with that, Pancho disappeared into the night, carrying the twenty dollars that Benson had paid him for the contact.

The electric window of the Cadillac came down, and a chubby Mexican leaned out. He didn't smile, but only reached behind him and opened the back door. Benson climbed into the rear seat and sat in the total darkness. There was no one else in the car but himself and the mute Mexican.

Benson began to grow edgy as the driver took him out of town and into the desert. The blackness around him, the hot winds, everything added up to give Benson a sense of real dread. He had never scored in Las Vegas before, had only heard about the place through the junkie grapevine. The stories that came out in Watts about the New Mexico town were incredible. Dope was easy there, no hassles and no pressure. The brown shit just floated across the border and into Las Vegas. After the shit went down in Watts, and a few of the brothers got on Benson for some dope hassles, the young Black had decided that new grounds were in order. Las Vegas was the perfect place. Loaded with enough smack, Benson took a Greyhound out of L.A. and rode with great expectations into the New Mexico desert.

But this first score was turning into something else again, and Benson didn't like the way it was coming off.

The Mexican stopped the car, pulling off the road into an open space. Benson bolted upright in the rear seat.

"Okay amigo. We make deal, now." The Mexican opened his door and stepped outside. Benson followed him from the rear.

The Mexican was much shorter than Benson, and Benson knew that if it came to it, he could take him. There was no sign that the little dealer carried a weapon, at least not a revolver, anyway. So Benson breathed a little easier.

"Fifty dollars, amigo," the Mexican said, reaching into his pocket and pulling out a small packet of the white stuff.

Benson took out his fifty dollars, wondering what the hell was happening. Standing out here in the middle of the fucking desert, making a small time score like this was far beyond his realm. He was prepared for anything, and if he wasn't so damned strung out for lack of the stuff, his adrenalin would have been flowing even faster.

The Mexican took the fifty dollars, then handed the small bag over to Benson. At that moment the sky seemed to explode. The entire area around them was lit up like the middle of the day. Benson froze, trying to adjust his eyes to the sudden explosion of bright headlights.

"Hold it right there, friend!" The voice carried the authority of the law with it. Benson recognized that sting immediately. He also recognized the fact that he had been set up. He believed that the little Mexican, along with Pancho, were doing nothing more than giving the local narcotics man his monthly quota of addicts; making the man's name a prominent one when promotion time came around.

"Aw fuck this shit, man!" Benson sighed as he saw the figure of a young Mexican walking toward him out of the glare of the headlights. By this time, the Mexican in the Cadillac had already gotten inside his car and was quickly disappearing down the highway.

"I'm Federal Narcotics Agent Tony Gonzia. You are under arrest for the illegal purchase of heroin. Your rights are as follows. . . ."

"Fuck that shit, man. What's the fuckin' trip?"

Agent Gonzia took the small packet from Benson, turning it around easily in his hand while he inspected it. "You need this stuff, amigo. You need it bad."

Benson didn't answer, but stood there watching the slim Mexican. Obviously he needed it, there was no other reason that he would be standing in the middle of the fucking desert if he didn't.

"You want it steady, amigo? You want to score anytime, and get paid for it?"

Benson couldn't believe what he was hearing.

The man was offering him the world. "Pull my coat to where you're coming from, man."

"Well," Gonzia began slowly, looking directly at Benson, "you got two choices. You either spend some time behind bars on this little rap here. Or, you work with me . . . as an undercover man."

"Oh shit, man!" Benson moaned. He had heard about the shit that came down on the undercover men who had been caught by the mainliners. It wasn't pretty.

"You got no choice, amigo. No choice at all."

Benson knew that the man was right. He would have to work for the law, something he had always detested. Benson shrugged his shoulders and stared at the desert sand.

Gonzia smiled, tossed the packet of heroin back to Benson and waved to someone in the car. "All right, man, let's get to work." Gonzia led Benson back toward the unmarked car. The desert winds blew hot and heavy that night, and William Benson rode in silence back to Las Vegas, New Mexico.

It was a long road from that hot night in the middle of the New Mexico desert; a road that would eventually lead the two men to the parking lot in the small town of Cloves.

Benson leaned over and held the door for his partner, who was juggling two hot cups of coffee. The black informer took his cup from the Mexican.

Tony Gonzia grinned as he sat down. "Why so grumpy, Will?" he asked, flashing his constant smile. "Don't worry, we'll find you another good connect.

William had to flinch at the insight of the Mexican. Tony had hit it right on the head. He wondered idly if he was that transparent. Then a flash of anger ran through him at the smugness of Tony. From the vantage point of his middle age he could look down at the hot shot agent. He knew if Tony stayed in undercover work, and continued to snort, he would one day be having the same problem.

"Don't worry about findin' me a good connect, Tony, worry about findin' a kilo pusher. That's what we get paid for," William stated, his dark brown features unreadable because of the lines of worry in his face. Fear, living with death, knowing in his heart that no informer could plan on tomorrow, had aged William.

Tony's round, friendly face never lost its smile as he changed the subject smoothly. "We have been feedin' our young friend long enough, but he's greedy, so he bears watching tonight," Tony said.

"All junkies need watching at all times, when money is involved," William replied quietly. He had his doubts about their young addict friend.

There was something sneaky about the brother they were dealing with. This would be the first time they spent a large sum of money with him. Before, he had only purchased fifty dollar bags for the undercover men, and then, he had only done business with William, better known as Will to the people in the streets.

"I could wish for a better connection myself," Tony said honestly, after taking a sip of coffee. "This fuckin' punk is playin' it too close to the chest. You watch and see. I can feel it. It just ain't right."

William shook his head in agreement. "Well what can we do? It's been played out to the limit, so what the hell. If this guy is going to introduce us to somebody big, it will be tonight, if not, we'll just have to let him go and try and find another junkie who can get us close to one of the bigger dealers in town."

"Yeah, I know," Tony answered quietly. "I get the royal ass because I know we can't come out and bust this punk we're dealin' with. It would blow our undercover work in this whole fuckin' city!"

"Uh huh," William agreed. "What time was that bastard supposed to show up here, seven o'clock, wasn't it?"

Tony glanced at the cheap Timex on his wrist. "Yeah, but you don't have to worry. He's got five more minutes, and you can bet your ass he's going to show up. Shit! You don't think he'll miss out on a free blow, do you?"

"I guess you're right," William replied, " 'Cause here comes slippery Dan now!"

Tony turned around and he could see the slim, dark-skinned Dan coming through the parked cars.

by Al C. Clark

He came straight to where the agents were parked.

Fat, round-faced Tony opened the door, keeping his idiot grin on his face as he greeted Dan. Even as the two men greeted each other, Tony thought about how nice it would be to take a vacation after this job was over. Maybe he could swing a deal where he could be looking for a heroin factory while he was in Mexico City. No, he had to give up that line of reasoning because the idiot role he played as an undercover agent wouldn't fit his real life identity. A smart young graduate from one of the best colleges California, four years of studying, then coming out and taking up the act of a grinning fool. To have to work with such a man as William was also something else, but it paid off in results. William had the knack for meeting drug addicts and having them trust him—something Tony had difficulty doing. He couldn't just ride into a strange city and that same night make a contact with some addict.

With William it was a simple thing, he could spot a user out of a crowd of people. Picking the right one on just sight alone, or so Tony believed. William never would explain how he knew who was an addict, and why he was sure the person he picked out really used.

"What it is, what it is," Dan said quickly, as he reached over and slapped William's palm. The two men greeted each other loudly, then as Tony closed the door after Dan got into the back seat, they lowered their voices.

"Is everything ready?" William inquired.

"It's as ready as I can get it," Dan answered quickly.

"What you mean by that?" Tony asked, ignoring the angry glare that William gave him.

"Hey, my man," Dan began, "what is this, quiz show U.S.A.? I mean, I'm supposed to answer so many questions for the sixty-four dollar jackpot, is that it?" He didn't bother to hide the sarcasm in his voice. Even though Dan did business with many Mexicans, he had never grown any large liking for them. But at least he treated them just like everybody else he came in contact with. He tried to take them all for a trick. Everybody could be beat in some kind of way. He believed all he had to do was wait and figure out where they were weak.

Without waiting for any directions, William started the car up and drove toward Sixth Street. He parked in front of a dingy, two-story building. "Hey, Dan," William began, "listen man, we want a piece of raw dope. We're willin' to spend nine hundred for it, plus toss in another hundred for you, so you ain't got to burn us. But we have got to meet The Man."

Dan waited silently until William had finished speaking, then stated, "I know what you want, Will, so I'll relate your feelin' to the man, but it ain't always what you want, if you want some good stuff."

by Al C. Clark

"Hey, my man," William began, "I thought all this crap was taken care of. When you told me to get the money together, and I told you I'd have to bring Tony along, you said cool. You said we could go in and test the dope right there. Now you act as if you want it to go some other kind of way."

"That ain't goin' be cool at all," Tony stated loudly. "It's got to go like you said earlier, it's too late for changes, not if I'm going to spend my money, anyway."

As Dan got out of the car, he shrugged his shoulders. It wasn't going as smooth as he planned, he reflected, but he had foreseen problems, and hoped that he had planned enough ahead to handle it.

"We will see what we will see," Dan stated, and walked toward the apartment building. Now, he hoped as he neared the building, that Emilio would have kept his part of the bargain so that things might still go off smoothly. Emilio Fernandez had been the only Mexican he could find who had the sense to pull this off. His brother Pedro was too hardheaded to work with, but Emilio was a horse of another color. He was chipping with the dope for one thing, so he was ready for anything that came along that might be smooth.

As soon as he entered the front door of the dwelling, he saw Emilio sitting on the stairway. "Hey, Dan, baby, am I glad to see you." The tall slim Mexican came toward Dan with his hand out.

"Is everything all right? Did the johns show up?"

Dan smiled at the Mexican. Emilio was boyishly slim, with dark eyes that matched the well groomed black hair that fell around his ears. His nose was well shaped, as well as the small mouth that made him seem feminine.

"Everything is all right so far, Emilio, except the motha-huppa's want to come in and test the dope," Dan stated, slowly stroking his chin as he tried to figure out a solution for their problem.

"Uh shit, man, I knew it was too sweet to work. Shit, five hundred dollars, man! Aw shit, sonofabitch! It was too good." Emilio stopped, thought for a moment, then asked, "Hey, man, why don't we stick the mothafuckers up? I got my knife, shit, man, if I'd only known, I could have stolen my brother's gun! Goddamn!" He was mumbling to himself.

"Listen, amigo," Dan said quietly. "Let's try it this way first. You step out on the porch with me. Then I'm going to bring one of the guys up here, just one, and you hand me—naw, better yet, you show us the dummy envelope we made up. Then you step back inside, sayin' you ain't goin' do no business with nobody but one of us. You know how to come down, man. Scream about the other dude sittin' in the car, cap on 'em that it's too many people involved. Next time if he comes alone, you'll do business with him. Now if he don't go for that," Dan added, "you tell us the hell with it, you don't need the money that bad, you dig? Turn your back like you don't want to waste no more time."

"I dig," Emilio said. "We goin' bluff this shit out, huh? To the bitter."

"Yeah," Dan said, and opened the door. "Hey, Emilio, I see that Preacher has got his Cadillac sittin' down at the curb, so let's walk down to the car like it's yours, you dig, and you fake like you're going to get in it. That should fake the motherfuckers out of their socks. With a new Caddie sittin' at the curb, it should relieve their minds about gettin' burned for their littl' bread. After all, they'll figure the car is worth more money than what they're putting up, so as long as they see the car, their minds will be at ease."

The two men walked down to the four-doored Fleetwood. "I would open the door and sit down," Emilio said, "but I think the Preacher has an alarm on the fuckin' thing."

"Yeah, man, you're right. It is one on it, so don't even shake the mother too hard. If the alarm goes off and we can't cut it off, it will blow our whole thing. Just fake like you're about to get in, then come back around and stand on the sidewalk. I ain't going be but a minute, so keep your fingers crossed."

"Okay, partner," Emilio said as Dan walked back toward the parked car where Tony and William waited. He walked around to the driver's side and motioned for William to roll down the window.

"Hey, Will," he began, "that's the Mex back there standin' beside his ride. He's thinkin' about ridin' off. He said fuck the deal. He didn't know there was going to be another stud in on it. He thought it was going to be just me and you, you dig?"

William glanced at his partner. "Fuck that shit," Tony began, "I don't want to see my money go out of my sight!"

Dan straightened up and shrugged his shoulders. "Okay then, Will, I'll tell the guy it's off. I doubt if we'll ever be able to get him to bring this much dope across town again. You know what I mean? It was almost too much for him to handle anyway, but he managed to get it up, now we go to Nut City on him 'cause we won't go along with his order that he don't want to meet a bunch of people at once. One person at a time is enough for him, and I don't blame him." Dan acted as if he was about to turn and leave. "I don't need no ride back, I'm going to ride with my man, back there. That new hog of his is mellow, and besides, he might just break one of his packages open on the ride."

"Wait a minute," Will said, this time not bothering to look at his partner, "maybe we can still work something out. You said he will meet me, didn't you?"

"Sure," Dan said quickly.

"Okay, okay then, let's go," William said and opened his car door.

Tony glared at his back. He didn't want to force himself on them because he might blow the buy. He felt the pistol in his shoulder holster At least they wouldn't be out of sight. He reached up and adjusted the mirror on his sunvisor so that he could see the three men without turning his head.

As the two men approached Emilio, Emilio removed himself from the fender of the car and met them on the sidewalk.

"Hey, Rico," Dan said, speaking to Emilio. "This is Will, I been coppin' for him for the past month. The guy is cool. We done shot up together five or six times. Ain't no funnies about him, he's a real dopefiend."

Emilio nodded his head in a way of greeting. "Hey man, ain't nothin' went the way it was supposed to have gone, Dan. What the fuck is that other stud doing in the car, huh? Wasn't nothing said about bringin' another guy around, man. I don't like strange shit like that, you know what I mean. I'd rather freeze on the sale."

"Hey, amigo," Dan began, "now don't you nut out on me. I'm tryin' my ass off to make everybody happy," Dan stated, glancing seriously at Will.

"Who's got the bread?" Emilio said sharply, taking Will by surprise.

"Why, oh, I have," Will answered shortly.

Emilio grunted, then removed the package from his inside pocket. He held it in his hand until Will pulled his wallet out. Both men were silent while Will extracted the bills from the wallet. Before he could count them out, Emilio turned on his heel and walked toward the front door of the apartment building. He stopped and turned around. "Hey man, I don't want to take nothing out of your hand. I don't know if your friend is takin' pictures of us or what. I just know he can't seem to stay still in the car seat from twisting around trying to see what we're doing!"

"Hey man," William said, helping his partner, "he's just worried about his end, that's all. You know, you can't put bread in everybody's hands man without gettin' burned."

"Shit!" Emilio cursed, "I'm used to selling kilos, not bullshit like this!" Emilio hesitated, then added, "you walk over to the side of the house and put the money down in the grass, then I'm going to lay your package down here beside the stairway. That way, ain't nobody did nothing, you dig?"

Will didn't like it, but he had to go along with it. If Tony moved fast enough, once Rico picked up the money they could still make the arrest. Will walked over and placed the money on the grass. He watched Rico place the white envelope beside the stairway, then walk toward him.

As Rico approached, William hesitated, then decided not to make the arrest until after he had picked up the package and had it in his hands. As he passed Rico, he made a small beckon for Tony to get out of the car. He motioned again as soon as he reached the package, but for some reason, Tony must not have seen him. He beckoned a third time as he straightened up with the envelope in his hand. When he glanced around toward Rico and Dan, he saw that both of them were gone. As he stared around stupidly, he heard the sounds of someone climbing a fence. He ran to the side of the house and was just in time to see Dan going over. He snatched his pistol out and started to fire, but caught himself before pulling the trigger.

"Goddamn it," Tony cursed as he came running up, "what the hell happened?"

William shook his head. "I made the buy, then beckoned for you three times to come on and help me arrest them, but you must have missed the signal."

"Missed hell!" Tony mumbled, "you sure in the hell must have went out of your way to signal me, 'cause I didn't see a fuckin' thing!"

"Well, at least we got the package," William said.

"Let's hope so," Tony growled. He took the white envelope out of William's hands and tore it open. He stuck his finger down inside it and tasted the white stuff on the end of his fingernail. He cursed and spit. "Goddamn it," he yelled as he gritted his jaws, "the bastard's sold you a thousand dollars worth of baking soda!"

William jerked the envelope out of Tony's hand and quickly tasted the stuff. He spit it out. He looked down at his partner while he struggled with his thoughts. Here he had been taken like a young punk who had never purchased drugs before. It hurt his pride as well as everything else. He couldn't look Tony in the eye.

"Goddamn it, it's going to be hell to pay for this, William," Tony stated. "I'm going to write in my statement that I didn't want to go along with it, and told you so. Yet you went against my wishes and still made the buy, even though there was the chance of us gettin' shit put on us!"

"It happens," William managed to say.

"Yeah, well you explain it to the boss," Tony answered, his eyes cold and bleak.

The two men started back toward the car, each one deep in his own thoughts. Tony worried about how this would look on his record, while William worried about whether or not the top brass would believe he was really beat out of the money. There were a lot of people in the office who objected to his even being on the payroll. It went against their sense of rights; an addict was paid a salary every week, and supplied with all the heroin he could ever use.

So why, he reasoned, should they think he would need the money when they gave him everything he wanted. There was no reason for him to beat them out of the money. Shit, they should be able to see that clearly enough.

"Oh hell, Tony, instead of us standing here like two fools, let's ride. Maybe we will be lucky enough to ride down on them," William said as he led the way back to the car. Any kind of action was better than none at all, he believed.

Tony followed with his head down. Things had really gone badly for them. Now they were going to ride the rest of the night like two silly ass fools, praying that the men that took them off would be as dumb as they had been. As he climbed into the car, Tony would have bet everything he had in the world against their chances of running into the slim Black man who had set them up so nicely.

After jumping the fence, Dan and his crime partner, Emilio, ran down the alley until they came to a vacant house. They ran through the empty back yard and came out on the next street. Emilio led the way as he crossed over and walked down the sidewalk toward another vacant yard. Again the men cut through the yard, coming out two blocks away from where they had begun.

As Dan brought up the rear, he searched through his pockets until he found an empty one. Then he quickly separated the money, not really knowing how much he took off the roll he had snatched up before Emilio could get his hands on it.

When they reached an alley, Emilio stopped.

97

"Hey, Dan, I think it's time we split up the money, okay? It looked like more than any five hundred dollars to me, my man. You wouldn't be puttin' shit on me, would you?"

Instead of answering, Dan removed the bankroll, minus the few hundred he had managed to remove to another pocket. "Hey, amigo, that's what's wrong with you guys. You don't trust nobody!"

"Yeah, man," Emilio replied. "I know just what you mean about us guys, but let's split the bread anyway, Honest John!" The sarcasm in Emilio's voice went unnoticed by Dan.

Dan pulled out the money and quickly counted it, while Emilio stared over his shoulder. "Hey, Dan, it's like I said! It's more than any fuckin' five hundred bucks there."

Dan nodded his head. "Yeah, Emilio, I counted seven hundred big ones, so let's make it three hundred and fifty dollars apiece. How's that for a few minutes work?"

"Shit man, it's sweet," Emilio replied, not really caring now if Dan had stolen a few dollars or not. Five hundred would have been a good sting for them, seven hundred was a dream. It was the best sting Emilio had made all year. Already he was planning on how he would spend his money. He reflected on his brother Pedro's warning for him not to mess with Dan. If he had followed his younger brother's advice, he wouldn't have made the three hundred and fifty dollars.

by Al C. Clark

Dan held the money out to the Mexican. For a second he thought about taking the whole thing for himself, but shoved the idea out of his mind. It would cause too much trouble, because he would have to almost kill the Mexican before he'd be able to get away with the money. Emilio wouldn't stand still for just a punk slap. No, he'd have to go all the way, and all he had on him was a knife, and he knew sure as hell the Mexican had a knife also.

"Okay, Emilio," Dan stated, giving the man his share of the money. "This should hold you for a few days, shouldn't it?" He was just making conversation as he tried to think of what would be his best move. Now that he had a nice bankroll, he wanted to make the money work for him. For the thousandth time, he wished that he could go straight to Fat George and cop. If he could, he'd be able to cop enough dope so that he could start dealing the shit himself.

"I'll be seeing you around," Emilio said as he began to slip away. He thought about ripping the tall Negro off, but decided against it. It would be too hard to do without a gun. The Black would fight like hell to keep his share of the money, so Emilio finally gave up the idea. If he had thought about it before, he could have set something up. Having a couple of his brothers waiting in an alley, then leading the Negro down that alley. But he hadn't been sure that the Black could pull the burn off. From the beginning, he had doubted the

Negro's word. He hadn't really believed that Dan had a live trick who would spend the kind of money Dan said he would. But it had come true.

Dan watched the Mexican walk away slowly, then he made his move. He didn't want Emilio to see which way he went, because he knew if the Mexican had any help, he'd try and rob Dan for the other three fifty. That was the way it was when you did business with dogs. You had to be prepared to defend yourself at any time because some kind of burn was sure to come your way.

Dan made his way through a yard that had a small white dog in it. The dog set up enough noise to wake up the neighborhood, but Dan was gone before the people inside the house could come out and see what the loud commotion was all about.

When he was sure he was far enough away so that he wouldn't have to worry about Emilio or any of his friends trying to hijack him, Dan stopped and lit a cigarette. He sat on the edge of a garbage can in an alley and smoked the cigarette down to a butt. At once, he snapped his fingers, then got up and made his way cautiously from the alley. Before crossing any well lighted streets, he made sure no cars were coming down the street.

It took Dan twenty minutes, but he finally made his way over to Curtis' house. After ringing the doorbell for about five minutes, he shook his head in disgust and started back down the stairway. Where the hell could that bitch be, he wondered, as he came back out on the street. He knew that he was going to have to cop some stuff from somewhere, but he had wanted to cop from Curtis. Curt had the best dope in town for a dealer pushing small quantities. Curtis didn't use, and for that one reason the dope was generally good.

As Dan stood on the sidewalk undecided on which way to go, a carload of drug addicts rolled up. One of them got out and came across the street. He stopped in front of Dan.

"What it is, my man," he yelled out as he came up and held his hand out for some skin.

"It ain't here, that's for sure," Dan stated, and enjoyed the look of disappointment on the man's face. As Dan stared at the addict, he tried to remember the man's name, but couldn't come up with it. The worried brown face that he stared at was a familiar one, but he couldn't place the junkie's name.

"Damn," the man said, then he broke into a smile. "I think I know where Curt is at," he said suddenly.

"Where?" Dan asked sharply.

"Down on Main Street, I believe," the addict answered. "When I was over earlier, his woman said something about Curt was going to take her out later this evening, but I didn't think they'd be gone this soon." The man started back across the street toward the waiting car.

"Hey," Dan called out, "how about giving me a

lift down to Main Street. I'm lookin' for the same thing you are." He crossed the street after the shorter man.

"You'll have to ask the driver, Dan," the man said, as they drew near the car. "I'm only ridin', Dan, it ain't my ride."

The driver of the old model car rolled his window down. He had already heard the conversation as the two men crossed the street.

"Hey, brother," Dan said as he approached the car, "how about lettin' me ride down on Main Street with the rest of you?"

The driver stared at Dan coldly. "Hey man, I ain't got no gas, but if you come up with a dollar or two, it will be cool with me."

Dan stared at him angrily for a minute. He knew the man was going right where he wanted to go, whether or not Dan went along with them. So it wasn't really a matter of gas. The man was just hustling for a little coin, that's all.

"Okay, man," Dan stated, not wanting to argue about a dollar since he had a pocket full of them. Any other time though, he would have talked the man into letting him ride along, maybe promising him some of the dope until after he copped. Then he would just disappear on the driver and not give him anything.

"Wonderful," the driver said, and held out his hand for the money before Dan could get in the car. As soon as Dan laid a dollar in his palm, he opened the car door and let him in on the driver's side. The other people in the car, three woman and three men, made room in the rear, grumbling about it at the same time.

Dan nearly got into an argument as he stepped on one of the men's feet climbing over a couple who wanted to stay near the window.

"Goddamn it man, why don't you watch what you're doing," the man yelled out loudly.

One of the women got up and let Dan have her seat, then she sat on his lap. As the addict who had gotten out of the car to cop got back in and delivered the news, a groan went up from the occupants of the car. Now they knew there was a chance that they might have to cop somewhere else that evening, and the idea of copping some dope from someone who used didn't appeal to any of them. As the car roared down the street, the thunder of the busted muffler drowned the disappointed grumblings of the people inside the car.

7

CURTIS WATCHED HIS WOMAN walk over to the jukebox. As he glanced around, he noticed he wasn't the only male in the crowded bar who watched Shirley's hips swaying under the tight-fitting black pants outfit.

Ruben Fernandez, the bartender, leaned over his bar and grinned at Curtis. "You got a pretty woman there, Curtis."

Before he could say anything else, the swinging doors opened and Fat George walked in, escorting his woman, Maria. She was a large, heavy-set Mexican woman who had once been one of the best prostitutes in the neighborhood. Then George got her and stopped her from working. Now, she came back to her old hangouts just to visit.

Maria waved around at the people as she made her grand entrance. She was dressed in an after five gown that was too expensive for the bar she was in. On her hands diamond rings glittered. She had on so much jewelry that it seemed to be phony, but the people who knew her and George realized that she wore the real thing.

"Hey amigo," George called out as he came near Curtis, "how's tricks?"

Curtis grinned at the fat Mexican. "You know about that better than I do, George, since you've got to hire a body guard to take your money to the bank."

George grinned, then waved to Ruben Fernandez. "Hey Fernandez, give everybody a drink on me." Then he took in the crowd of people at the tables and changed his order. "That is, the ones sittin' at the bar." He smiled brightly and looked at everybody.

As Shirley came back from the jukebox, she embraced George's wife in the middle of the floor. Maria's loud voice could be heard over the blare of the jukebox. "My, Shirley," she shouted, "it seems years since the last time I saw you." They both knew that she had been over to Shirley's house only two days before, making a drop for George.

Curtis moved over, making room at the bar for George. "How has business been going, George?" he inquired pleasantly.

George shrugged his shoulders. "Some days a

man can't make a dollar, it's best to stay in bed."

"In your case, a dollar means a few thousand, huh?" Curt asked, making conversation.

As the two men chatted back and forth, Ruben went up and down the bar, pouring drinks for the customers. When he finished, he came back down and stood in front of George. "Was that invitation for the bartender, too?" he asked, knowing beforehand that he was welcome to a drink at George's expense.

"Yeah, Ruben, as long as you don't drink no phony ass colored water and charge me for the best whiskey in the house!"

Ruben smiled, then removed a bottle of Johnnie Walker Red from the back of the bar. He poured himself a stiff drink, then pouted out another one for George.

As George tossed off his drink, Curtis leaned over and whispered in his ear, "I'm thinkin' about buyin' maybe a half a kilo, George. That is, if I can get the right price."

"Hey, amigo," George replied, "with me, you always get the right price, and the best jive in the city. Right?"

There was no guile in Curtis' voice as he answered. "I'll give you your proper, George. Since I've been dealin' with you, I ain't had no reason to complain. Everybody who cops from me seems to like what I give them." Curtis stated honestly, then added, "as long as I stop short of the number of cuts you say I can put on my jive."

"What you mean, Curt, stop short," George inquired, smiling all the time.

"You know," Curtis began, "if you say the stuff will take a five, then I put a four on it. That way, I always have the bomb. If I was to put the whole five on it like you say, my stuff would just be ordinary, you dig?"

George shook his head. "Maybe you've got a point there, but the joint I run across town, we don't get no complaints there, and I put the whole fuckin' five cut to the mess that I drop off there." George put his empty glass down and pointed at it after catching Ruben's eye.

Ruben had backed away from them so that he wouldn't appear to be listening to what they were talking about, even though everybody in the bar knew that both of the men were dope men. The word was spreading on Curtis. It was whispered around that he was on his way to becoming a big pusher.

"Fill mine up and put something in Curt's glass too," George ordered as the bartender came up carrying the bottle of Johnnie Walker.

After filling the drinks, Ruben started to back away, but Shirley and Maria climbed up on their stools. "Bring us a bottle of that bubblin' stuff," Maria called out loud enough for half the bar to hear her.

The four people watched as Ruben expertly

popped the top off the champagne. "Any of you gentlemen want to indulge?" he inquired, as he shook ice cubes around in a glass until the glasses were cooled. After pouring the drinks for the women, he came down to the men, holding the bottle in front of him. "Well?"

"Shit, Fernandez, you know I don't drink nobody's fuckin' wine," George stated.

"I'll take a glassful," Curt said softly.

As Ruben poured out the drink, Curtis caught the eye of an addict who had just come in the bar. The thin, light-complexioned man stood at the doorway, glancing around coldly at all the people enjoying themselves. His enjoyment would come out of the end of a needle, if he happened to be lucky enough to make a good buy instead of some of the junk that was being sold for dope.

Curtis caught the man's nod and got up from the bar. "I'll be right back, I got to go to the littl' boys room," he said as he left his small party at the bar.

The addict waited until Curtis was almost to the men's room before he moved slowly in that direction. George knew at once what was happening, but doubted if Ruben did. Ruben wouldn't stand for any dope selling in the bar when he worked his shift. That was the reason the rear door had been closed and blocked off by beer cases. The young pushers in the neighborhood had started selling stuff right out of the back door. They would hand the stuff over to the various addicts, then the addicts would continue right on out the back door.

Curtis was back in a minute. He climbed up on his stool and picked up his glass of wine. "Damn, that felt good, I feel like a new man," he said loud enough for the bartender to hear.

The high-pitched sound of Maria almost drowned out his words as she laughed at something Shirley had said. Another record dropped on the jukebox and couples began to push out on the small area that was marked off for dancing. It was just a little circle that was between the tables. There was no stage for a band to play on. The bar was just a small neighborhood joint where a person could come and sit and drink.

The crowd was a mixture of soldiers from the nearby base, and a large amount of Blacks with just a sprinkling of Mexicans, mostly in mixed couples. Next door was a club that catered to the Mexicans in the neighborhood. The jukebox there carried mostly Mexican music, so it caused a lot of Negroes to bypass the club. That was exactly what the owner wanted.

Outside of the club, the car with Dan and the other drug addicts pulled up. As Dan got out of the rear seat, he glanced up just in time to see the car carrying Benson and Tony in it. When he saw them, they had just noticed him.

William slammed on the brakes. Before the car came to a complete stop, Tony was jumping out with his pistol in his hand. Dan glanced over his shoulder and saw the fat Mexican with the gun in his hand. In his panic, he forgot that he couldn't get out the back way of the bar, and ran through the front door. As soon as he entered, he realized his mistake.

Dan spotted Curtis and Fat George sitting at the bar. He ran over to them instantly. His mind was working like lightning. Maybe, just maybe, he hoped, one of the dope men might have a gun on them.

"Curt," he said, gasping for breath, "I had to run ahead, man," he managed to get out. "There's a couple of studs comin' in here man, who plan on stickin' up the bar, so that they can knock off you and George. I mean it, man, I didn't want no part of it when I heard about them plannin' on knockin' you off, Curt." As he spoke, sweat broke out on his forehead. "I mean, as long as they were talkin' about just Fat George here I didn't give a shit, but when they included you, Curt, I had to draw a line."

Ruben had moved up as Dan spoke, and reached under the bar. "There won't be any stickups in my place," he warned.

Fat George was trembling visibly. His fat cheeks shook with fear.

"To put the icing on the cake," Dan added, "you better hide your money somewhere. They'll be coming through the door in a second, Curt." He backed up quickly, trying to hide next to the doorway.

The first one through the swinging doors was Tony, his police special was in his hand. As he came through the doorway, he stopped and blinked, trying to focus his eyes in the dimness of the bar. Before he could adjust them, Ruben swung the shotgun he held onto the top of the bar and pointed it at the man in the doorway.

Before Tony could reply, Ruben's nerves caused him to pull one of the triggers. The force of the shotgun blast lifted Tony off his feet and slammed him back against the swinging doors. He would have gone through them if it hadn't been for his partner, William, who was just entering the bar.

William saw the man behind the bar with the shotgun. He knew instantly that something had gone wrong. As his partner fell into him, he tried to shove the body away, then saw the man with the shotgun swinging the gun around at him. He raised his .38 automatic and fired off a wild shot that miraculously struck the bartender in the chest, slamming him back against the bottles.

Tony's body slipped and fell to the floor just as the mortally wounded bartender raised the shotgun in his bloody hands and pulled the other trigger, "Oh, my God," William managed to say before the force of the buckshot struck him and slammed him back through the doorway. He struck the ground and rolled over. For a minute, he couldn't figure out what had happened. As he rolled over and tried to sit up, he saw a dark figure come out of the bar and run down the street. Something in the back of his mind flashed, but he couldn't figure out why the retreating figure of Dan should mean anything to him. That was his last thought as the pain in his chest became unbearable and he slipped into the growing fog of darkness, never to awaken again.

"Goddamn, goddamn," Fat George murmured over and over again.

Curtis went behind the bar and held the head of the dying bartender. "Did I get them?" Ruben inquired, his voice barely above a whisper.

"Yeah," Curt said, as a lump came into his throat, "you damn sure did get both of them, Ruben." He wondered why the death of a man who meant nothing to him should affect him the way this one was doing.

"Good! Good!" Ruben said, "I told you wasn't no bastards goin' come in my bar and stick up nobody, didn't I?"

"You sure as hell did," Curtis answered softly as he felt the man's warm blood running down onto his hands.

"The nerve of them bastards, Curt, comin' in here with guns. . . ."

Ruben the bartender never finished what he was about to say. His head dropped to the side and he died.

Basketball practice lasted until twelve-thirty that

night. Billy and his club had practiced well, they were getting it together with their fast break, a move that had held them up during all of their previous games. Billy was the guard, and when the tall, lanky center Edgar got his rebound, Billy was the man to whom the high post bullet came. Edgar and Billy had been practicing this move for weeks, and this night the practice was paying off.

"Hey man, that's smooth. Beautiful!!!" The small, fat coach shouted after Billy had sunk his sixth straight fast break lay-up.

Billy grinned at the coach, then ran back across the court and slapped Edgar's hand. The two boys had dreams of someday making it into the college ranks, then maybe to the pros. They both knew that they had talent, and both were trying their hardest to realize their potential.

"It's goin' good, Billy," Edgar said, throwing a towel around his neck. "We got ourselves something here, my man. We just might make it!"

"You and me, Edgar baby! You an' me!"

They showered and dressed, slapping each other in the locker room and joking constantly. They all felt good, they were doing something that they liked. And then there was the added fact that playing basketball might lead them out of the slums and ghettos and into a decent life. Each man on the team had the same dream, and each man had the same vision of what he would do if that dream were to come true. For Edgar, it was getting

his little sister and brother out of Cloves and into
some decent house, paying for their education and
maybe some new clothes.

For Billy, he thought of getting his mother away
from her small house. Maybe out to the ocean to
live like human beings some day. As far as Curtis
was concerned, Billy knew that his older brother
would never accept his money, anyway. So there
was no reason to even think of giving him any. But
the dream felt good, it made him respect his body
and his mind. He knew that as long as he continued
to play ball he would never fall into the pits that
he had seen so many of his brothers fall into. Dope
would never catch him, as long as he could make a
fast break and sink a lay-up.

"Hey, man, how about comin' over to my place.
We could catch the tape delay of that Lakers'
game?"

"No, Edgar, not tonight, man." Billy was just
finishing pulling on his old sweater. "I got to get
home and get some sleep, man. It's been a long
day."

Edgar smiled at his friend. The two were like
brothers, traveling together down a road that they
both knew would end somewhere better than
where they had started. "Okay, man. Don't want
you gettin' jealous over West or Goodrich or any of
those other dudes, right?"

"Hey man," Billy joked back, "last time you
saw Jabber we couldn't get you out on the damn

court for a week. All you could say was 'mannnnn . . . nobody ever goin' beat that dude!' "

The two youths shadow-boxed each other, laughing and dodging at the same time.

"You never be a boxer, boy," Edgar chided.

"An' you never be no Cassius Clay, neither!"

The locker room had emptied. Most of the other guys had wanted to get away from the smelly gymnasium where they practiced. Edgar and Billy were always the last to leave. To them, the place was like a dream—an escape from reality where they could build themselves a life.

"Catch you tomorrow, man," Edgar called out as they split up outside the gym.

"Right, man! An' keep on thinkin' you're shooting that ball from a cannon!" Billy watched the tall, lanky figure of Edgar disappear around the corner of the building. He turned and started toward his mother's house where he knew a good helping of black-eyed peas would be waiting.

Through the dark alleys and vacated streets, Billy moved with the grace of an athlete. He thought about the moves that he had made that night. He thought about Edgar, and the obvious improvement the big man had made over the past few months. It was incredible to him, but the idea kept coming back into his mind. Both he and Edgar were going to make it! They were good, the best twosome in the area, and because of them their team could beat anybody around. It would be a long way to the pros, but Billy, for the first time in his young life, was beginning to believe that he and Edgar would really make it.

His daydreaming continued as he crossed Sixth Street and started the last, long block toward his home. He didn't see the shadowy figure cross in front of him down the street. Nor did he hear the sound of boot heels on the cement behind him. He was oblivious to everything but his dream of making it as a professional basketball player.

"Hey nigger!"

Billy stopped. It wasn't the first time he had heard the word. But the voice was familiar. He came instantly out of his daydream. Pedro Fernandez! It was his voice, that high sounding twang that had so many times drifted through his bedroom window when Curtis and Dan had been shooting craps with him out in the back yard.

"Hey niggerman! Your blood brothers out to wipe the Chicanos, man?"

Billy stood on the sidewalk, not knowing where to turn. Pedro had never come at him before. As a matter of fact, Pedro had never come at any Black man before. It was not like him to pick a fight with a Black.

"What's happenin', Pedro?" Billy yelled, hoping that maybe Pedro had mistaken him for someone else.

"You tell me, brother, 'cause I ain't got no more brothers, you dig? I mean, that nigger Dan made sure that Ruben got laid under, you dig?"

"Pedro, what are you talking about, man?"

"C'mon, man. Be cool. You know what the motherfuckin' truth is!!!"

Billy felt the adrenalin begin pouring through his system. He still couldn't see anyone. But the hysterical pitch of Pedro's voice told him that something was wrong. Something had happened, and he was getting blamed for it.

"You motherfuckin' nigger!!! You'll all pay with your cocksuckin' black hides!!!"

Billy knew that it was time to run. He spun around on his heels and started in the opposite direction of Pedro's voice. But the dark figure of Jay, a Mexican friend of Pedro's, stopped him.

Pedro ran out of his hiding place and came up behind Billy. In another moment, Carlos Montoya, the biggest dude in the Chicano section of Cloves, was there also. Billy stood in the middle of the three men, with nowhere to turn.

"Okay, pequito bastard! You shall pay in Hell for Ruben!!! You goddamn little nigger!!!" Pedro was hysterical, Billy could see that much. His eyes were filled with tears, and his fists trembled in a rage that would not be easy to control.

"Hey man," Billy pleaded, "be cool. I been playin' ball all night. I don't know nothin' 'bout nothin'!"

Pedro Fernandez did not let Billy finish his own defense. He threw a right into Billy's hard stomach.

It was a strong enough hit to force Billy over. Pedro came down instantly across the back of Billy's neck, flattening him onto the sidewalk.

Billy lifted himself to his knees, then up onto his feet. He gasped for air, the breath had been knocked out of him. He tried to focus on the men standing around him, but his eyes were watering terribly from fear and pain.

"Carlos, show the motherfucker what it means!"

Carlos looked at Pedro, then at Jay. He grabbed Billy by the shoulders, bending him backwards, and then raised his knee to Billy's lower back.

Red exploded in Billy's brain. The air rushed out of him, his body seemed to melt in an explosion of pain. He felt himself slipping backwards onto the sidewalk and could only listen numbly as his head hit the pavement with a sickening crack.

Pedro stood above the helpless body. He placed the heel of his boot on Billy's groin and added pressure. Billy screamed, but never even heard his own cry of pain and terror.

"The man's a chicken shit, Carlos. Look at him. He'll never play basketball again . . . eh, amigos?"

Carlos and Jay laughed. Pedro continued to exert pressure onto Billy's balls. Billy screamed out, and Carlos finally figured out how to stop the sounds. He stuffed an old oil rag into Billy's mouth.

"All right, the bastard will never do nothin'. Maybe the fuckers will learn a lesson!!!" Pedro was half in tears as the three men dragged Billy's tortured body back amongst some trash cans. They moved the cans in front of Billy so that no one would see him from the street.

"Maybe," Pedro began before they left the scene, "just maybe the nigger will come to work sweeping out my house, eh?"

The three laughed. As they started to walk away, Jay, the silent, stone-faced one of the group stopped. He slowly pulled a .38 revolver from his coat, and walked back toward the body.

Pedro and Carlos watched as Jay, without hesitation, fired a shot into Billy's back. The limp body on the ground twitched, then fell into silence. Jay placed the pistol back into his coat pocket, turned to Pedro and said, "Like you said. man, he'll never play ball again."

The three men ran quickly back toward their homes.

Billy lay half paralyzed in the alley. He would spend the night there, sinking always into the dark abyss of his tortured madness until finally someone would find him the next morning and get him to a hospital.

It wasn't until morning that the news spread that the men Ruben had killed had been police. Then the stories began to fly. They had run into the bar after a junkie to arrest him for something or other, nobody really knew what. But one thing was sure, they knew the two officers were chasing after a drug addict, and before daybreak the addict's name was all over town. Even the police knew who the man was, only they didn't know where he was at.

Across town in a small, brown-framed house, the Fernandez family gathered. It was early in the morning before the story reached them about the two policemen their older brother had shot. After that, they began making calls on their old telephone which hung on the wall. The ones doing the calling were the younger brother, Pedro, and the angry Emilio, who knew at once who the junkie was the two policemen were chasing. He blamed himself for his older brother's death. But more than himself, he blamed Dan, for running into the bar telling the lie he had obviously told.

Before daylight arrived, Fat George came by the Fernandez house with his wife, Maria. They both told the tale of how Dan had run into the bar and swore Fat George and Curtis were about to be robbed and how Ruben swore nobody would get stuck up in his bar.

The two brothers cursed loudly, while their mother and sister cried. The two Mexican women held each other and cried in each other's open arms.

Pedro had reacted the night before, but didn't tell Emilio about his actions. He wanted more blood. Ruben had been like the father to the whole family, supporting them off his earnings ever since

the day he had left school after their father's
death. Sometimes he had worked two jobs so that
there would be enough food and good clothing in
the house for all the kids. The younger members of
the family weren't asked to do anything but to
continue on in school.

The only thing that Ruben wouldn't tolerate
from any of his brothers or sister was skipping
school. He had an idea that if they got good
educations, they would never have to work at
share-croppin' like their father had done. He hated
farms.

Now that Ruben was dead, the old gray-haired
mother of the family stood in a state of shock. She
couldn't believe her oldest child was dead. They
hadn't brought the body home, so all she had to go
on was the word of other people. True, she had
sent her sons down to see the body and they came
back and told her it was Ruben. She still didn't
want to accept it. Sarah, her daughter, had been
sent back to the city morgue with Emilio to see the
body. When she came back with the same report,
Mrs. Fernandez had broken down completely.

After telling everything he knew about the death
of Ruben, Fat George dug into his pocket and
removed a hundred dollar bill. On a second
thought, he pulled out another one and left two
hundred dollars on the table beside the old woman.
George couldn't look her in the eye. For some
reason, he felt that she thought he was responsible

for the death of Ruben. He quickly left with his wife on his arm. For once, Maria's voice was low and subdued.

Once outside the house, Maria spoke. "I hope they catch that lying sonofabitch for causing this family all this grief!"

"Don't worry," George said quietly, "it will be taken care of, and if the police don't move quick, there won't be nothing for them to arrest."

"That's good, Georgie," she said, using the name she always used when she was thankful for something he had done for her.

George seemed to be speaking to himself as he continued. "Yeah, that nigger is a dead man. Even if the police do get him, he'll die in prison, you can lay odds on it, and be makin' a sure bet all the time!"

Maria patted his fat arm as he opened the door for her. If George said it would be taken care of, she didn't have to worry about it any longer. It would be taken care of.

8

IT WAS A BEAUTIFUL DAY. The morning music by the singing birds came through the open window, and you could smell the warmness and brightness of the day in the air.

Curtis rolled over and tried to cover his head with a sheet, but the sunshine still came through. It wasn't really the hot sunshine that he was trying to hide from, he just didn't want to face the day. The past night's work was too much for him, it was still too stark raving clear in his mind. He could still feel the blood of the dead man on his hands, even though he had almost rubbed his skin off trying to wash the blood when he had come home that morning.

"Honey," Shirley's voice drifted to him from the kitchen, "would you like a large breakfast this morning, or just some black coffee?"

"Coffee, dear," Curtis called back, then kicked the sheets off and climbed out of his bed. Curtis raised his arms and stretched. He could smell the morning's fresh air, yet he took no enjoyment in it. What he had tried not to think about came rushing back to him.

After slipping on a robe, Curtis went into the kitchen. "Honey," he began, "what you want to do today? I'm going over to Mom's pad in a little while, so if you want to, you can gather up the kids when they come home for lunch and take them along."

Before answering, Shirley set a cup of coffee in front of him. "Curt, I got all that washin' to do, baby, so I better stay home and get it finished. Maybe later on this afternoon when you get back I'll be finished and we can ride out to a park or something."

Neither one wanted to bring up the killings. They talked around the subject. Finally, Shirley sat down at the kitchen table beside Curtis. "It ain't no use blaming yourself for what happened Curt. Dan is just a no good bastard, that's all."

"Yeah, I know. It's easy to tell yourself that, but people think me and Dan are closer than what we really are," Curtis said softly as he slowly sipped his steaming coffee.

"Shit!" she exclaimed. "You're not responsible for what another nigger does, daddy, so don't worry yourself over it!"

124

They were suddenly interrupted by the ringing of the doorbell. Shirley got up quickly and went to the door. She didn't bother opening it, but just glanced through the peephole.

"Ain't nothing happenin', dear," Curt heard her say. Then she added, "I don't know how long it's goin' be, maybe a day, or sometime tomorrow. But it ain't goin' be no time soon, so don't come back in the next couple of hours."

She came back to the kitchen shaking her head. "At times I feel sorry for them addicts. Then another time I don't give a shit what happens to them. I know one thing, Curt, they will worry the fuckin' shit out of a person about that goddamn dope!"

Curtis nodded his head in agreement. "Yeah, honey, I know they get on your nerves, but try not to be too mean to them when you speak. I mean, we do live quite good off them, so we have to put up with them. At least, until we get where we don't have to deal in such small packages, then the money will be bigger and everything."

"I ain't worried about the money, Curt. We're gettin' more money now than I've ever believed possible. It's just that dopefiends are just so goddamn dangerous! Look at that shit Dan pulled off. You never know what's going to happen when you deal with them kind of people, that's all."

Curtis looked at her. "Honey, if you feel thata'way about it, maybe I can set up something different than what we are going through right now."

"Like what, Curt?" she asked curiously.

"I don't really know offhand, Shirley, but if I could find some guy who I could trust, I'd put a bag in his hands, or better yet, I'd rent a place for him to live and sell the jive out of."

"It sounds good, Curt, but can you find somebody who you can put that much faith in?"

He tossed his hands in the air. "Ain't no sense of worrying about all that mess right now, Shirley, 'cause I don't even know when I'll be able to cop again. After that shit last night, fat ass George is frightened to death of niggers."

"Well maybe it's all for the best. We got a small start, Curt. If you got a job for a few weeks, with the check I get, it would be enough for us to get along on," Shirley stated.

Curtis got up from the table. "Let's not start on that shit, girl. A job is for a lame, and I don't want no part of it!"

Shirley whirled around and slammed some dishes down in the sink. She didn't bother to answer him again, but she showed her disapproval by her actions. Curtis ignored her, and went back into the bedroom. As he dressed, he thought about what she had said and laughed. He was used to making two, maybe three hundred dollars a day now, and to go back to a job would be like giving up. He liked the recognition that went along with getting big money, as well as the money itself.

The telephone rang sharply in the front room. Curtis listened with one ear as his woman answered it. "Curt, it's for you," Shirley called out.

He picked up the phone in the bedroom. "Hey, what is it?" he inquired as he reached for a smoke.

"What!" he yelled suddenly, forgetting about the cigarette he was reaching for. He held the phone close and listened quietly, then he asked one question. "Which hospital is he in?"

Shirley came into the bedroom and watched Curtis as he held the telephone close to his ear. He hung up slowly, a vacant look in his eyes.

"What's the matter?" she asked, sensing something was wrong, even though she didn't know what it could be.

"It's my brother," he began. "Some Mexicans caught him coming home from the gym and jumped on him. I ain't got the full truth about it, but it seems as if they thought he knew where Dan was hiding out. How fuckin' stupid can a goddamn person be." Curtis cursed angrily. "How the fuck would Billy know any fuckin' thing about Dan?"

"You want me to go to the hospital with you?" she asked after a moment of silence.

"Naw, baby, that won't be necessary. You stay here and take care of the kids. As soon as I hear something I'll call back and let you know."

Shirley followed him to the door, and held it open as he went out. "Okay honey," she said, as she stood in the doorway, "don't forget to call either way. I want to know what's wrong with Billy as bad as you do."

Curtis ran down the stairway, and when he reached the front door of the modern apartment house, he almost collided with an elderly man who lived in one of the downstairs apartments.

Curtis continued to run after sidestepping the old man, until he reached his old car. He started it up and drove swiftly away. When Curtis reached the hospital, he didn't waste any time searching for a place to park. He just pulled up beside a red line painted on the curb and parked.

The Martin Luther King hospital was used mostly by the poor Blacks and Mexicans in the nearby communities. As soon as Curtis reached the in-patient waiting room, he began to look for his mother and sister. The hospital waiting room was full of Negroes waiting for friends and relatives. As Curtis made his way up to the desk, he could smell the odor that only a hospital carried.

The round-faced Black nurse behind the desk glanced up at Curtis with a bored expression on her face. "Yes," she inquired in a high, thin voice that he would have never guessed came from a woman with so much bulk.

"I'm here to see about my brother who was brought in earlier. His name is Billy Carson. I think he was. . . ." Before he could finish, she interrupted him.

"Oh yes, you're asking about the young man who was attacked near the high school." Her face became serious and there was compassion in the look she gave him.

"He's not hurt seriously, is he?" Curtis asked sharply, shaken by the woman's open concern.

"I'm afraid he's still in intensive care, but you can go back to room 104 and find out more. I think your mother is already back there, young man," she said as he turned to leave.

Curtis walked down a long hallway until he saw a sign with the room numbers. He turned right and began passing patients laying on stretchers. A group of people were sitting next to a doorway and as he passed, he saw that it was the x-ray room.

The people sitting on the benches outside the x-ray room watched the tall, well dressed Black man as he went past. There was something about his bearing that made people look at him a second time. It was not because he was slim and supple, all bone and muscle and sinew. What caught their attention was the brutal leanness about his face. He looked like a hawk hunting its prey.

As soon as he made another right turn, closely following the directions, he saw his mother staring wildly up and down the hallway. Tears were streaming down her dark cheeks as his sister stood helplessly by.

"Momma," he heard his sister say as he walked up, "it's goin' be all right. It could be worse."

Rita, looked over her mother's shoulder and saw her brother coming toward them. A look of relief flashed across her features as she saw him.

"Momma, here's Curtis now," she said, hoping to give her mother some relief, but the words only had the opposite effect.

Mrs. Carson whirled around on her older son with fury blazing from her eyes. "There you are! I don't know why you bothered to come down here! Maybe it's just to see what kind of handiwork your gangster friends did to your brother. You ought to be ashamed to even show your face down here!" Her voice was loud and hysterical as her emotions got the best of her.

Curtis was taken by surprise by the anger of his mother. He felt it was uncalled for. He hadn't done a thing to deserve it.

Her words continued to beat at him, even though Rita tried desperately to shut her up. "It's all your fault, it wasn't Billy they wanted, it was you! But since they couldn't find you, they took their anger out on him. Now he's layin' in there, unable to move, because of you!"

The words 'unable to move' shook him more than her senseless anger. "He ain't paralyzed," Curtis asked, bewilderment and shock in his voice.

Rita shook her head. "I didn't tell you on the telephone, because the doctors hadn't finished checkin' him out yet. But the men who jumped on him also shot him while he was layin' on the ground. One of the dirty bastards shot Billy in the back!'' Tears began to flow down her cheeks.

Oh my God, Curtis thought angrily, it was all becoming like a nightmare. Why? Why? Why? The words kept flashing through his mind. It couldn't be because of him. Curtis thought back and knew he hadn't done anything to any Mexicans to make them want to take their anger out on him. So why was Billy attacked?

"Why?" He didn't ask the question to anybody in particular. The word just came out.

"Why, why," his mother screamed in his face, "because of that no good sonofabitch that you had over to the house a few weeks ago. The bastard ate at my table! Now this has happened to my boy!"

Dan! The name came and went in Curtis' frantic thoughts. "You mean because of that nigger Dan?" He looked at Rita.

Rita nodded her head. "Billy said they thought he knew where Dan was hiding out. When he couldn't tell them where Dan was, they jumped on him."

Curtis heard what she said, but he didn't want to believe her. Could it be possible for somebody to be that foolish. To make him responsible for what somebody else had done. It was possible. The more he thought about it, the more he was sure that Pedro and his wild bunch of hoodlums were responsible for this. It would be like the foolish young Mexican to do something stupid, make somebody else pay for something that they didn't have anything to do with.

"Momma," he began.

"Just shut your mouth, boy! I don't want to hear no excuses now. Your brother is layin' in there, ruined for life because of you. So why don't you just go on back from where ever you come from. We don't need you here, Curtis, just go on." She never considered the pain she was causing her older boy. Her words beat at him like falling bricks. As he listened to her, a feeling of terrible shame overcame him.

"Momma, why don't you stop that," Rita said as her anger grew. She didn't hold Curtis responsible, and hated to hear her mother talk to him like that.

Curtis' eyes were filled with pain. As he stared at his mother, a feeling of great depression overcame him. He couldn't do anything about what had happened, it was done and over with, but he could make the people responsible for it pay. And he meant to make them pay dearly. At first, he had felt pity for the Fernandez family, but now, there was no pity in his heart. His mother's words beat out any pity that he might have had for anyone. Now, there was only the thought of revenge. Not only on the Mexicans, but on Dan, who caused all of it to happen in the first place.

"Rita," Curtis began, "I'm goin' take off. It ain't nothing I can do around here. With Momma feelin' the way she does, it ain't no reason for me to hang out here, but I'm going to take care of the matter. The people who caused this are going to pay, and don't think for a damn minute that they ain't! I just want you to know that I ain't done nothing to nobody to make them do this thing to Billy."

"I know," she answered quickly, "but you take care of yourself, Curt. Momma is just upset right now. After she gets used to it she will realize that it wasn't because of you that it happened. I'm just sorry that she carried on the way she did, that's all." Rita spoke truthfully, trying to remove some of the pain she saw in his face. Her mother had been very unjust as far as she was concerned. But when it came to mothers, you couldn't tell them anything. You just had to go along with them, even though a lot of times they were wrong.

"Call me at my house when you leave, okay Rita," Curtis asked as he started to leave.

She nodded okay, then watched him as he turned on his heels and left. There would be hell to pay somewhere in the city, she knew, because Curtis wasn't the kind of man who took abuse lightly.

9

"WHAT THE HELL DID YOU SAY YOU DID?" Emilio Fernandez yelled at his younger brother.

"I said we caught that spade, Billy, coming from school and kicked the shit out of him," Pedro replied.

"Why?" Emilio asked, as he sighed and sat back down on their aging couch. His mother and sister had left home earlier to go to the funeral home nearby to leave a proper suit for Ruben.

"Why?" Pedro repeated. "We wanted the coon to tell us where that punk Dan was hangin' out, that's why."

"Brother, just stop for a minute and think. Billy don't even run around with his brother, Curtis, so why pick on him. He wouldn't know where Dan was hangin' out, because they are two different kind of studs. Even you, Pedro, should be able to realize that."

"All these spade dudes know about each other, Emilio. You just like to hang around them too much 'cause you're shootin' that fuckin' shit now!" Pedro eyed his older brother angrily.

"Bullshit, Pedro, and you know that's all it is. You just wanted to kick the shit out of somebody, and he happened to come along. I guess you figured it all out, 'cause when you have trouble with Curtis, don't come runnin' home telling me all about it."

"I don't give a flyin' fuck about no Curtis, man! To me, he ain't nothin' but another burr-head," Pedro replied arrogantly.

As Emilio stared at his brother, he had to shake his head in wonder, because he knew Pedro meant what he said. Here he had gone out of his way and angered one of the meanest studs in the city, and Pedro didn't give a shit about it. As he stared at his brother, he had second thoughts, because in the back of the dark eyes that stared out at him, he could see the hint of fear there. His brother was just putting on a big front while shaking in his pants.

"Okay, Pedro," he said, "It's your problem, I got my own troubles to worry about. It's too much trouble trying to live, without going out of my way gettin' in some silly ass gang fight. You and that fuckin' bunch of Chicanos that you run around with are going to bite off more than you can handle one of these days!"

Pedro laughed harshly. "I'm not about to lose no sleep on account of no nigger, Emilio, even if you do." Pedro stood up and began to pace.

"You ain't shittin' me," Emilio replied. "I know damn well you're worried, and you should be. Curtis won't take this lightly, but maybe if you guys didn't hurt his brother too bad, we might be able to get Fat George to hush it up."

For a few seconds Pedro didn't bother to answer, then he stopped his pacing. "Listen man, he was hurt bad. That dumb ass Vic Mohica shot him in the back while he was on the ground."

"What?" Emilio roared, jumping up from the couch and snatching his brother's arm. "You mean Billy was shot too?" Emilio couldn't believe it, he didn't want to believe it.

"Just hold on, Emilio. I tried, I honestly tried to stop it, but it got out of hand. You know how these things are in a street rumble."

"Street rumble my ass," Emilio growled. "What kind of street rumble is it when six or seven guys kick the shit out of one kid. Street rumble. Bullshit!" Emilio started to pace, then snapped his fingers. "Jesus Christ, we let Momma Mia and Maria go to the fuckin' funeral home without no protection. Goddamn," he yelled, as he ran towards the front door.

Pedro followed closely behind his brother. "Hey, Emilio, don't you think you're carrying this thing a little far. This stud wouldn't do nothing to our mother."

Emilio whirled on him. "You stupid bastard, if you fucked his brother up for nothing, do you think he gives a shit about our mother or sister? All he wants is black vengeance, and that means he'll strike at whoever the hell he can!"

As the two men hurried down the sidewalk, their mother and sister were getting ready to leave the funeral home.

Curtis sat across the street from the Old Spanish Funeral home. If he had it figured right, some members of the Fernandez family would have to show up some time today. He glanced in his mirror as a car turned down the lonely street and drove slowly past. Curtis wiped the sweat from his brow. His only worry was the license tags he had removed from another car and put on top of his. He fingered the sawed-off shotgun, then leaned it against the window sill. His face had taken on a cruel snarl that belonged to the past—on some jungle hunter. There was no mercy at all in his expression.

As he sat waiting, he could still hear the words of his mother beating at him. It was a shame that things had to turn out this way, but he couldn't let the Mexicans get away with it. If they did, there was no telling who they might attack next. His best bet was to knock off the remaining two brothers. That way, he wouldn't have any more trouble out of the Fernandez family, because there wouldn't be any of the males left to worry about.

As these thoughts flashed through his mind, he saw the funeral parlor door open and two women come out. As he looked closely, he saw that it was an old woman and a girl. As they drew near, he recognized Maria, the young sister in the Fernandez family. That must be the mother with her, he reflected, as he hesitated briefly. He didn't want to make war on the women, but he wanted to strike back so that they would be as hurt as he was. He sighed as the women drew nearer, then he slowly raised the sawed-off shotgun and held it on the window frame. As the two women came abreast of the car, he pointed the gun directly at the young girl, then pulled both triggers. The roar of the gun almost deafened him, but he still managed to get the car in gear and pull away from the curb.

Young Maria took the full blast of both barrels. The shotgun knocked her into her mother with such force that she pushed her mother off her feet. The buckshot ripped open the young girl's side all the way up to her armpits. Blood spattered the older woman who still hadn't figured out what had happened.

As she managed to push her daughter off of her, she climbed slowly to her feet, then leaned down and shook her daughter. At the sight of the blood, she let out a scream that was far louder than the noise the shotgun blast had made. People came running from all directions to help, and in the crowd were her two sons.

by Al C. Clark

Emilio took his mother in his arms. He held her tightly, as he stared down over her back at the body of his baby sister. Tears of rage filled his eyes as he glanced up at his brother who was looking at the carnage dumbfounded.

All Pedro could do was shake his head. "I never figured it would get out of hand like this," he murmured to himself, unaware that he was actually talking out loud.

"You sonofabitch," Emilio cursed as he clutched his weeping mother in his arms. "Now, goddamn it," he cursed at the sky, "I'm goddamn sure in it!"

Pedro was so shocked by what he saw, he could only bend over his sister's body and cry. "It's not my fault," he cried over and over again, until somebody took him by the arm and led him away. He never knew who it was that led him to the funeral home and sat him down in a chair. He couldn't see because of the tears that ran so freely down his cheeks.

Curtis drove six blocks before stopping and removing the license plates off his car. He then drove to an empty alley and broke the shotgun down. He left a piece of it in a burning garbage can, then drove farther and tossed another piece away. Each time he made sure the piece he tossed away was cleanly wiped. The killing of the young girl didn't bother him, though. He was numb from the pain of the early morning incidents.

Before arriving home, he stopped and called, giving Shirley plenty of warning not to allow anybody inside the apartment until after he got there. She listened quietly to his orders, then hung up.

Curtis climbed back in his car and drove slowly home. His whole world seemed to have changed in less than twenty-four hours. It was hard to figure, but he knew now that nothing would ever be the same. He realized also, that he had another job to do. There was no way he was going to allow Dan to get away with the shit he had started. Somebody had to make him pay for it, and Curtis felt in the mood to be the one to do it.

The thought flashed through his mind, as he drove aimlessly for a minute, that he would have to purchase another gun. It would have to be a gun that couldn't be traced back to him. He gave the thoughts free roaming time, and soon he knew right where to go to find the kind of weapon he needed. He pressed down on the gas. But first things first, though. He wanted to make sure Dan was where he thought he might be, then he'd get the gun. It wouldn't take long. Dan wasn't that hard a man for him to find, especially when he was so determined.

10

IT WAS STILL TOO LIGHT OUTSIDE, Dan thought as he stared moodily out of the vacant house window. Even though Dan hadn't occupied the empty yellow house long, there was plenty of evidence that revealed that someone had taken up temporary shelter in the deserted home.

The floor of the once clean and well kept home was now littered with debris that Dan had scattered about. Empty pop bottles and cigarette packs were everywhere. "Goddamn," he murmured to himself as he stared out the window, unable to make up his mind on what to do. One thing was for sure, he moaned, as another stomach cramp hit him. It was past time for him to fix. If he didn't

want to become a real sick junkie, he would have
to get out of the deserted house and find some
junk. But from who? The question came back to
him for the thousandth time. Who in the hell could
he turn to? It was impossible for him to just walk
up on the set and cop. There would be a hundred
police up there minutes after he arrived. No, he'd
have to come up with something a hell of a lot
better than that. Dan reached for another cigarette
only to find the pack was completely empty. He
tossed it on the floor, cursing under his breath.

Dan began to pace. He was like some wild ani-
mal who had been caged too long. He thought of
Curtis but rejected the idea as soon as he had it.
Curtis wouldn't do a damn thing to help. The only
thing he could depend on was that Curtis wouldn't
turn him over to any fuckin' police. Dope, dope,
dope, that was the all important thing right now.
Nothing else meant a goddamn thing. He had to
find some drugs and it would have to be done
soon!

This time when Dan started for the rear door he
didn't hesitate. He glanced out of the boarded up
window before slowly pushing open the back door.
The late afternoon breeze felt good on his face as
he walked quickly through the rear yard. As he
jumped the fence, he saw three young Negro kids
playing in the alley.

"See, I told you," one of them called out to his
buddy.

by Al C. Clark

"Told me what?" his friend asked quickly.

"I told you somebody was living in that old house, remember?"

The other colored child shook his head. "That don't prove nothin' 'cause he jumped the fence. He might just be cuttin' through the yard."

"Hey Mister," the young kid yelled as he ran after Dan, trying to prove his point, "don't you live back there?"

Dan glared angrily over his shoulder. "Ain't your momma taught you to mind your own business nigger!" Dan cursed, and continued to walk swiftly down the alley.

The other boy laughed at his friend's predicament as he ran up. "You ain't proved nothin'," he sang as he reached them.

"You young punks better go and find you somewhere else to play," Dan warned them sharply as he glared at them out of his swollen red eyes.

Neither child was a fool. First of all they knew Dan was a young man, and that meant that he outrun either one of them. That one fact was more than enough for them. They both turned on their heels and went back the way they had come, every now and then looking back to see where the tall dark man was. The second time they turned around, Dan had disappeared. They realized at once that the man had taken a shortcut through one of the back yards farther down the alley.

Once out on the street again, away from the

alluring feeling of security the alleys gave him, Dan became overly cautious. He took his time before venturing out from the sidewalks and crossing the narrow streets. He wandered aimlessly at first, hoping that he might just run across some addicts that didn't know him that well. He knew that he was only fooling himself, because even if he ran into that unlikely addict, the junkie would know from grapevine that Dan was running.

As he neared Fifteenth Street he still hadn't made up his mind on which direction to take. He stopped in the middle of the block and just stood there with his hands on his hips. He was the picture of rejection at that moment. Here he was, he reflected, with a damned pocketful of money and nowhere to spend it. The sight of a small neighborhood grocery store caught his searching eyes. He quickly crossed the deserted street and entered the store. Dan glanced around, then picked up a cold bottle of orange pop. He stayed in the store and drank the pop slowly as the aging male storekeeper watched him closely.

Before leaving Dan bought a small cake. He didn't really want anything to eat at that moment, but he decided to force himself to eat something. There was no way of knowing when he might get the chance to eat again. This goddamn running shit, he decided, was for the birds. Once again the idea came to him that his best bet would be to leave town. Yet, even if he caught the bus out of

by Al C. Clark

town, he'd still have to find some dope before he left. There was no way possible for him to even think about leaving unless he had an ample supply of drugs.

As he took a quick look at the street before venturing back out again, he anxiously rejected one addict's name after another until he couldn't think of anyone that used. He started quietly going back over the names in his mind again. With the realization that there was no one he could actually trust finally making itself completely understood, he began to seethe with anger. Not at himself for being the sole blame, but at others for being so dishonest a man couldn't put any faith in them.

Well, well, old buddy, he said to himself as he made up his mind on what to do, if the mountain won't come to Mohammed, Ol' Moe here will just have to go to the motherfuckin' mountain. As he walked, he talked to himself, moreso to build up his own courage than for any other reason.

After finally making up his mind on what he was going to do, it didn't take Dan long to reach his destination. When he reached Tenth Street he turned down the alley. The house he sought was in the middle of the block. At first, he didn't recognize the back yard that he was looking for, but the broken down fence at the rear of the house was the one he was looking for. Dan moved slowly to the rear of the house. It would have appeared to an observer that Dan was expecting an attack, rather

145

than approaching a house whose occupants rarely bothered themselves enough to care about someone else's problems.

The mother of the home had a drinking problem as well as the father while the son, who Dan was seeking, had a drug problem.

Dan ducked under an old clothes line and knocked softly on the rear window. After waiting a second, he knocked again. This time, he hadn't long to wait before he heard some noise from within.

Suddenly the ragged window shade flew up and a light, pimple-faced Black man stared out at him. Dan watched the man's face closely. Instantly it began to change. At first the man didn't seem to know who it was, but when he recognized Dan he changed. First, his light brown skin took on a dark shade that could only come from the blood rushing from his heart. Next, but just as transparent, was the hugeness of his eyes. They appeared ready to jump out of his head.

"Hey, baby boy," Dan said in a more cheerful voice than he felt, "you look as if you done went and seen you a ghost."

For a while, all the man could do was stand and stare opened-mouthed. "Goddamn, Dan," he said finally.

Before he could say anything else, Dan cut him off. "Listen Milton, I want you to do something for me, man."

This time it was Milton who did the cutting off. "Dan," he began, raising his hands up in a show of hopelessness. "Man, you're so goddamn hot a man could fry an egg on your shadow, brother! I mean, just for lettin' certain people know where they could reach you would be worth at least a bill, man!"

"Is that all?" Dan said coldly. "Shit, for a motherfucker takin' the risk of puttin' the finger on me, it's worth his motherfuckin' life, so add that shit up and tell me is a funky hundred dollars worth a cocksucker's life!"

Milton shook his head quickly, fear was showing in every pore of his body. A person standing next to him could actually smell it coming out of the little man.

"Aw brother," his voice had changed into a high whine, "I was just tellin' you what's being said Dan, that's all, man. Somebody ought to pull your coat to what's going down, if by chance you don't already know."

"Naw Milton, I'm up on it, but as you can see, ain't nothin' happened yet, 'cause the people who was goin' cross me ain't able to ever cross anybody else now."

Milton just stood and stared at him like a frightened rabbit. "Man!" he managed to say.

Seeing that the man was truly frightened, Dan decided the time was ripe for him to make his offer. "Dig, Milton, you look as if you need a fix."

147

Dan waited until Milton nodded his head in agreement before continuing. "Okay, now money ain't no problem, Milton, but I'm havin' trouble coppin', as you probably already know."

Again Milton nodded his head in agreement. He couldn't think of a pusher who would be foolish enough to do any kind of business with Dan. But he didn't waste any words stating this fact. As he managed to get his nerves under control, Milton glanced at Dan's face for the first time and quickly realized that the tall dark man was sick. Up until then, it hadn't even occurred to him to wonder why Dan would pop up in his back yard when half the city was out looking for him.

It had been too much like a bad dream. Dan spelled trouble. Anybody caught with him would more than likely catch the same kind of hell Dan was going to catch whenever the right people ran down on him.

"Man, I ain't got no stuff, Dan," Milton mumbled, then added, "I mean, you know if I had anything I'd set it out for you, but I ain't fixed since this morning."

Dan waved his excuses away. He knew that if the man had a kilo inside under the bed he wouldn't give any of it away. He was a petty nigger and always would be. "Listen, Milt, I didn't come over here to beg, boy, I come to get you to go and cop for me." Dan waited, trying to read the frightened man's mind. When Milton didn't comment right off, Dan asked, "Did you hear what I said, boy? I want you to go cop for me."

Milton had heard all right, he just hadn't finished going over the alternatives that it left. If someone should get hip to the fact that he copped for Dan his ass would be in a sling. But on the other hand, he wanted a blow and if he didn't go and cop for Dan, he didn't have the slightest idea of where he would be able to raise the money to get a fix.

"It's takin' you a long time to make up your mind about somethin' that simple, Milt. Now, if by chance you're going over the idea of burnin' me, or some other self-destroyin' thoughts like that, you'd be better off if you went inside and wiped out your mammy or paw, 'cause that's just what the hell I'd do if I even thought you were going to do something that might cause me trouble!"

"Naw, Dan," Milton said hurriedly. "I was just tryin' to figure out who had some good jive. Since Curt's brother got hurt, he ain't had no stuff."

"Well, I was thinkin' about spendin' at least a hundred dollars. That is, if you knew where some real good jive was. But," Dan warned, his voice dropping down into a cruel growl, "I don't want no motherfuckin' bunk, and I ain't acceptin' none neither."

"Naw, Dan, if I go cop, you ain't got to worry 'bout no bunk, man. I been around too long. Nigger got to be out of his mind to even think

149

'bout selling me some bunk.''

Dan kept his eyes on the young man's face. He knew what Milton said was true. Milton had mud on his name, so people were leery of taking his money unless they had some good dope to sell him. There were rumors out about Milton having dropped dimes on pushers who put shit on him. If a pusher took his money and sold him some bullshit, when Milton came back and demanded his money they set it out, or closed up shop, because if his money wasn't returned you could expect a visit from the police sometime soon.

Dan tried not to show his urgency, but it wasn't possible for him to hide it. It was in his voice when he spoke. "You think you might be able to cop some decent scag, man?"

Milton knew he had a fish on the line, yet at the same time he understood the dangers of handling what he had hooked. "Yeah, Dan, it ain't no problem me coppin', but where you goin' be when I come back?"

The question didn't take Dan by surprise, but it did cause shivers of fear to run up and down his spine. "Don't worry about where I'm going to be. You just don't take long going to cop. I'll be somewhere watchin' whenever you get back, just don't stay gone over an hour."

Milton sighed. There wasn't nothing he could do but cop, then hit the package before leaving the dope house, and take whatever Dan gave him when he got back. That should be enough to hold him until tomorrow anyway. Be happy to get that much out of the deal.

"Listen," Dan added, "it's twenty-five dollars extra in this for you, Milton, so hurry on up. If you take care right, who knows, there will be other times."

As Dan spoke, Milton smiled at him and shook his head, but he knew if it was up to him, there wouldn't be any more times. Not after this one. Dan was just too hot to fuck with. Milton couldn't keep the greed out of his eyes as he watched Dan remove the large roll from his pocket. His eyes stayed glued to the money. Just maybe, he reflected, he might be able to squeeze one more cop in after all. Since no one knew about it, it should go as sweet as cotton candy, with no after effects. Dan wasn't in any position to go and tell anybody about who was coppin' for him, and the last thing in the world Milton would do would be to allow even a rumor get out that he had helped Dan out.

"How long you goin' be?" Dan asked as he held the money out to Milton.

"Give me about thirty minutes, Dan. It shouldn't take any longer."

"Okay, now you remember what I said, Milton. If any kind of cross comes out of this shit, somebody real close to you will answer for it until the day arrives that you can pay for your own mistakes. I know how easy it is for you to think that all you have to do is stay out of my way until somebody catches up with me, but you better hide your whole fuckin' family, man, 'cause I'll burn this stupid ass house down with them in it!"

"Aw, Dan, that ain't no way for friends to talk, now is it? If you want, you can climb through the window and hide out inside in my room until I come back," Milton said seriously. "That should show you I'm for real with you, Dan."

"That don't prove shit to me, Milton. You might leave, and plan on callin' back while you're gone and tell them to get out. Or, you might try sending the motherfuckin' police. But whichever, I'll kill the stink on shit, boy, if you cross me, you understand?"

Milton was shaking openly, and as he realized that Dan wasn't going to accept his invitation to enter, he relaxed. Anything might have happened while he was gone. And then his family would have been under the gun all because he tried to be for real with a nigger. No, it was much better that the man laid across the street or somewhere—anywhere other than Milton's home.

Before Dan could change his mind Milton began to close the window. He dropped the shade quickly as he suddenly recognized a look of indecision flash across the tall, dark man's face. It had suddenly occurred to Dan that he might just be doing the best thing if he stayed in the man's bedroom. There were so many things on his mind that he just couldn't think of everything at once. Even though he understood his mistake instantly.

As Milton disappeared from view Dan began to glance around the yard, trying to take in as many advantage points as he could. The best place, he reasoned, would be across the street. That way, if something funny did come up, he wouldn't be trapped as easy as he would be in Milton's back yard.

Dan re-entered the alley and walked until he found a back yard that wasn't fenced in. Even though someone lived in the house, the yard was easy to walk through. He had almost reached the house when an elderly woman came out. "Here, there, young man. This ain't no open highway, boy. People live in this house!"

For a second Dan thought the woman was going to try and block his path. He didn't have any time to waste because he wanted to be out front whenever Milton came out of the house. First, he wanted to know which way the man went when he drove off. Next, he didn't know what kind of car Milton drove. It was all important knowing which kind of car the man drove away in.

His luck was good. As soon as he came out of the old woman's yard, he saw Milton entering an old dark green Ford. He stood with his back against the hedges until the car pulled away from the curb. He was so involved in watching Milton that he ignored the elderly woman. The word police brought him back to his present problem.

"I'm sorry ma'am," he began, hoping to fake her out with kindness. He pointed at his ears. "I ain't able to hear too good, ma'am."

"I don't give a shit whether or not you can hear or not, boy, but if you don't get on 'bout your business and get off my property I'm goin' do like I said and call the police on you. Your kind is always sneakin' about, tryin' to find somethin' to steal!"

Goddamn this noisy bitch, Dan cursed inwardly. She could blow the whole thing for him. "Miss Lady," he began, "I ain't no thief, no matter what you think. Hell, lady," he said and pulled out his roll of money and flashed it at her, "I don't have to steal from nobody, 'cause I got a damn good job workin' for Mr. Jackson. Yes ma'am. I works each and every day," he said, putting his money away.

From the look of greed that flashed across the old woman's face, he knew she wasn't about to call no police. The woman was too busy wishing she was younger so that she could remove some of that cash from a young fool who didn't know what to do with it.

Dan removed a cigarette from his pocket, then pretended as if he couldn't find a match. As he fumbled around dumbly, he saw the look of cunning and disappointment in the woman's face.

"I'll give you a match, boy, but I got to go inside the house to get one," the woman stated, then as she turned to go, Dan put out his bait.

"Miss, I'd gladly pay you if you would be kind enough to bring me a cold drink of water out with you." He smiled broadly. What he wanted most of all was the chance to stay on her porch, so that he could watch up and down the street. Maybe, just maybe, he prayed, he might be able to con her into allowing him to sit there.

As soon as she entered the house Dan walked up on the porch. He sat down quickly on the old brown chair that was there. It was a torn rocking chair, and as Dan began to rock, he wondered idly if the thing would bear up under his slight weight.

He didn't have long to wait before she reappeared carrying a tray with two glasses on it. "Since you mentioned pay, I didn't want to charge you for no water, so I fixed up some ice tea," she said, then laughed loudly.

Dan noticed that she hadn't wasted any time before mentioning money, so he decided his best bet would be to give her something at once. Then he could lead her on about some more if the need should arrive. Taking his time, Dan slowly removed the bankroll he had and quickly slipped a dollar off the bottom of it. He honestly hesitated over the amount he gave her. At first he started to give her two dollars, but it seemed as if that was too much for such a small thing. He held up the dollar as he pushed the rest of the money back into his pocket.

"Here, Miss," he said as he took a quick swallow

of the almost sugarless drink, "this sure beats drinking water on a day like this."

She took the dollar greedily from his hand, while a look of disappointment flashed across her face. It was quite obvious that she had hoped for more, but for the life of him, Dan couldn't figure out why in the hell she thought she deserved it. Not for the damn-near bitter ass drink she served him.

"Young man," she began, "you'd be surprised at what things cost nowadays. For a woman my age, it's almost impossible to live."

Without taking his eyes off the conniving woman's face, he decided to make it hard on her, to see how far she would go. Since she was too old for sex, he wondered idly just which way would she try and con him out of his bread. He could tell from her earlier reactions that she definitely wasn't satisfied with the dollar. But hell, he thought, he couldn't for the life of him see where she was coming from. If he hadn't needed the use of her porch, he'd have quickly told her to kiss his ass, the scheming old bitch!

None of his thoughts showed as he stared earnestly into her face. "You just wouldn't believe it," she stated again, "just what it takes for an old woman like me to get along on nowadays. I mean, I can make it, but if I should want a drink, now that's something that has to be put off until the first—" She caught herself in time, or so she thought. She had been about to mention the first of the month when most elderly people got their old age checks, but through her cunning, she thought that it was best if she didn't mention when her money came.

She hesitated briefly, then gave her phony little laugh and continued, "yeah, we have to wait until the first good-hearted person comes along and feels sorry for us and buys us a little something." Her little birdlike eyes darted at him, to see if he was getting the message. She continued after briefly giving her brittle laugh. *"He he he he he,"* the sound of it was loud and shrill.

Dan tried to not hear it. He imagined an open tunnel, but no parts of his imagination could cover up the aging teeth that were revealed as her mouth opened wider and wider. The sound seemed to continue forever until for a minute he thought he was about to lose his mind.

After about ten more minutes he wondered if he wouldn't have been better off if he had gone on to the alley across the street and found a vacant yard.

"Here son," the woman croaked, her shrill voice now raising the hairs on his arm. "Have some more. It ain't often that Aunt Jeanny goes and finds her such nice young company. Nowadays young people don't want to be bothered with us old folks, but I could see at once that you was of a different kind. Yes sirreee, right off, I could tell that you was like they use to be. Ain't many of the children raised thata'way nowadays. No sirreee, you just don't find them like that any more." Her voice continued to go on and on, while Dan wondered if she would ever stop.

He closed his eyes and wished that the voice would stop. How he'd like to slam something into it!

"Boy, son," he opened his eyes and found her leaning down over him, "son, you sleepy or something? You don't look quite right. Is somethin' botherin' you?"

Goddamn right it is, he wanted to scream out at her. This motherfuckin' jones is killin' me, woman, but the words wouldn't come. At least, he didn't allow them to come. He doubted whether or not they would even shock the old woman anyway.

"No, no," he answered quickly, "I don't care for any more tea." He had to smile to himself. He hadn't known the goddamn difference. The shit could have been piss for all the shit he knew.

Dan glanced up the street wildly, hoping that at any moment he might see Milton returning. He cursed under his breath. No such fuckin' luck. He let his mind drift, ignoring the pleading old woman beside him.

This would have been a wonderful place for him to hide out, he reflected, but after a few days around the old woman, he'd be mad. Other than that, it would have been as if he had disappeared.

"Now, if I only had about eight dollars to hold

me . . . Aunt Jeanny began, but was interrupted by the actions of her company.

While the woman had been speaking Dan had closed his eyes again. When he reopened them, the first thing he saw was Milton parking his car. He watched Milton glance up and down the street, looking for Dan in his hiding place. After carefully examining the street, Dan stepped off the porch, catching the woman in mid-sentence. He didn't bother to glance back as he took the first two steps on the jump.

The old woman stared open-mouthed at the departing figure. "You stingy sonofabitch!" she yelled at him. Whether or not he heard her she couldn't tell because he never bothered to look back.

Before Milton climbed the last steps to his front porch, Dan was at the sidewalk that led up to his front door.

"Hey Milton," he called out, "how 'bout you slowin' down for a minute?"

Milton stopped on the porch. A look of shock flashed across his face. Dan could tell that the man resented him coming out in the open. The very first words Milton spoke proved him right.

"Goddamn, Dan, I thought you'd at least meet me in the rear, not come running up to me out on the goddamn street!" Milton glanced quickly up and down the deserted street. Even though he didn't see any one he couldn't relax. "Why don't you cut through the yard, man, and I'll open the back window."

"Fuck that shit," Dan growled, as he reached in his pocket and removed his money. He quickly removed a twenty dollar bill and a five. "Where's that fuckin' package?" The question was more like an order.

Milton didn't have too much nerve from the beginning, so he quickly reached down into the front of his pants and removed the bag of dope that he had concealed there within his Jockey shorts. Before handing the dope over, he reached out and got the twenty-five dollars from Dan.

"How we goin' do this, Dan? I was going into the pad and split the dope. I just wanted a small amount out of it anyway," Milton pleaded. He watched Dan concealing the drugs on his person.

"What you talkin' 'bout, man?" Dan asked, all the time being aware of just what Milton wanted. He didn't even bother to wait for an answer, but turned on his heels and started back down the way he had come.

Milton came down the steps on a run. "Hey, Dan, what's the deal, man?" he cried, as he tagged after Dan, not caring now who saw him.

"Hey man, I gave you some cash, Milton, you can run back and cop you another bag of stuff."

"Yeah, I could do that, Dan, but that ain't the way it's supposed to be going down. You said when I got back that we was going to get loaded off this motha-fucker, not nothin' 'bout me going back and recoppin' with the twenty-five dollars. Shit, Dan, you done promised me the twenty-five motherfuckin' dollars just for going and gettin' down for you!"

Without bothering to look back at the shorter man who had to run to keep up, Dan lengthened his long stride.

The sight of a young Black boy on his paper route caused Milton to hesitate, but the thought of losing out on all the dope pushed him on. "Come on man, let's go back to my crib and break down the drugs like you said from the get."

Dan stopped in his tracks. "I guess you ain't goin' get the message no other way, Milton, but I ain't givin' up none of this bread, man. If you ain't happy with what you got, it's too motherfuckin' bad, brother, 'cause you ain't 'bout to put none of this jive in your veins!"

Milton stared at him hotly for a second. "Okay Dan, if that's the way you goin' do it, I got to go 'long with it. But mark my words, nigger, one day you'll want me to cop again, and I'll remind you about this funky shit you pulled off on me today!"

"You just do that," Dan snapped back at him. "If I should get in the shape I was in earlier today, I need you to remind me about myself, you punk ass nigger!"

All Milton could do was stare angrily at the taller man. If he had been able to, Milton would have tried Dan, but he knew he didn't have it trying to fight the bigger man.

"Okay, Dan, I deserve what you did. When you lay down with snakes, you should expect to get bit!"

Dan only laughed as he started walking away. If he could have seen the look on the paperboy's face he wouldn't have taken it for such a joke. As Milton turned to leave, he saw the young boy push his bike out into the street and start peddling it slowly. He was going in the same direction as Dan.

11

FAT GEORGE MOVED AROUND THE HOUSE quickly.
For a man his size, it was unnatural. Sweat ran
freely from his brow, but it didn't stop him; if
anything, it added speed to his packing. Bags upon
bags were now sitting at the door, awaiting the
moment when they would be picked up and taken
out to the waiting car.

"Goddamn it woman," Fat George cursed,
"can't you move your ass any faster?"

Maria looked out around the doorway from inside the kitchen. "I don't know why the hell we
have to rush so, George. If I listen to you, we'll end
up leaving half our fuckin' stuff right here."

"If you don't hurry the hell up, I'm going to do
just that, leave all this shit for somebody else!"

"Well if you do, I'll be that somebody, George,
because I done told you I'm not running away and
leaving my stuff!"

"Shit!" The word seemed to explode from him. As he set his last bag down, George leaned against the doorway. The apartment was large and expensive. It was easy to see why Maria had second thoughts about leaving. The furniture was the latest in modern. The couch was deep gold with a matching pair of heavy armchairs. The thick carpet on the floor was a dark shade of forest green. The throw rugs that ran criss-cross on top of the carpet were some of the most expensive that money could buy. The long heavy drapes that were still hanging from the windows were again done in the rare gold color that Maria had found. She had had the drapes shipped to her all the way from Mexico City.

"If you want something to do, George," Maria called out, "why don't you start taking down the damn drapes. That way, you'll save me a lot of trouble."

"Drapes hell," George roared from the doorway, "I don't seem to be able to get through to you, Maria. We have to get the fuck out of here. Not this afternoon or later on this evening, but now!"

"Shit, George, I'm asking you again, what the hell is the rush? Maybe if I knew why, then I could go 'long with this shit, but as long as you keep me in the damn dark, it ain't nothing serious about all this hurry hurry hurry shit of yours!"

George let out a sigh. Maybe it would be better if he let her in on it, he reflected. Then she would be able to understand the importance of it and by *Al C. Clark*

hurry the hell up!

"Listen Maria," he began. "Maybe it would have been better if you knew. That phone call I got this morning, honey, was a warning. Somebody told those silly ass Fernandez brothers that I sold some drugs to Dan and Curtis. Now you and I know this ain't nothing but bullshit, but they don't."

"The Fernandez brothers," she drawled. "Who the hell are they but a punk named Pedro and his goddamn brother Emilio. Is that the reason why you're running scared? Goddamn, George, get some backbone! My God! Are we supposed to allow two would-be gangsters to run us out of our homes?"

George let out a sigh. "You don't understand, woman. It's not just the two brothers, there's a fuckin' war going on between the Chicanos and the niggers, and if the Chicanos should get the idea that I'm helpin' the spades out, goddamn woman, do I have to spell it out for you?"

Maria came out of the kitchen. Her hands were on her hips in an attitude of anger. "It still ain't nowhere as near as bad as you make out. George, you're Mexican yourself, so am I. Do you think our people will think we are going against them? Hell no, not for one minute! I know them better than that, and you should too."

"Yeah, any other time I'd go along with what you say, but the phone call Maria, the person who took the chance on calling me, knew what he was talkin' about! Right now can't anyone make reason to Pedro, since his sister got killed. He won't listen to anybody. So should I stay here and try and reason with a fool?"

"Well, you should do something. You got enough money to hire some people to handle guys like Pedro. So why run?"

"That's just it, I don't want to hire people to handle Pedro, then everybody will think I'm really on the side of the niggers. No, Maria, that's what I don't want. If somebody had to hurt Pedro because of me, it would look bad. So, I'll do the next best thing. I'll get the hell out of town for a few weeks until things die back down. It shouldn't take long, that's why I say to you to leave most of this shit. It will be here when we get back."

"Okay, okay, George, but what about the way people are going to talk when they hear that a young punk like Pedro ran you out of town?"

"It's not Pedro we're running from, Maria, it's those crazy ass punks who run around with him. Every one of them is out to build up a rep, Maria, and I don't want them to get one off of me!"

"Okay, George, I understand now, but I still think you're going about this wrong. At least you should have had the fuckin' sense to hire some kind of protection for us. If it's as dangerous as you say, shit, we need a fuckin' bodyguard right this moment."

"If you'd quite running your fuckin' mouth and

do like I ask, we won't need anything but your ass helping to lug these fuckin' bags out to the car. Come on Maria, we can be in Mexico before daybreak if we get a good start this evening."

As he spoke, George reached over and opened the door. Maria was in the middle of leaning down to pick up two of the bags when she stopped suddenly and froze. "Oh my God," she murmured softly.

George didn't have to glance around her to know what was happening. It was all like a bad dream. Ever since he first got the telephone call, it was as if he was on a stage watching other people act out their parts. No matter what he did, he didn't believe he could change what was about to happen.

"Well, how about this shit, Emilio," Pedro said as he came through the door. "Our little nigger lover was about to fly the coop. What's wrong, George, ain't the spades got any more money for you to suck out? Or by chance did you learn that we had heard about your constant dealing with them, after you were warned not to fuck with them for a while." Pedro's arrogance was obvious to all watching.

12

REALIZING THAT IT WOULD BE a waste of time trying to reason with Pedro, George ignored him and
spoke directly to Emilio.

"Emilio, I don't know how your brother came
up with his fucked up ideas but he's wrong as
usual. I ain't had no dealings with them spades,
man. The last time I sold some drugs to them was
before your brother Ruben got killed!"

The words were hardly out of his mouth when
Pedro reached over and knocked George to the
floor with a straight right to the head. "You nigger-
lovin' bastard," Pedro panted, "don't let me hear
you using my brother's name in your filthy mouth

again, you understand?" There was a wild look in his eyes and as George glanced up from the floor at him the thought flashed through his mind that the young bastard was completely crazy. It came as a shock to George. He had known that Pedro was wild, but he really had nothing to do with him before. This was one of the few times they were ever in each other's company.

"Emilio," George called from the floor. "Listen to reason man, don't make a mistake that both of us will be sorry for."

There was a look of indecision on Emilio's face. From it George got a ray of hope. Before he could go on though, Pedro nodded his head and another Mexican came in and then slammed the door shut.

"Vic," Pedro spoke to the Mexican who had just shut the door, "what do you think, should we shoot this bastard, or maybe cut him up a little?" Pedro's voice was now soft, barely heard by the people in the room.

Maria spoke up. She knew the other Mexican who had come in with them. "You, Jay Novello, I know you and all your family, now you know me, too. Would I lie to you, Jay?" She didn't give the young man a chance to respond, but continued, "even though this shit you guys got going with George doesn't concern me, I want to speak up. Jay, you tell them if I'm lying, hear?"

Pedro attempted to shut her up, but her voice began to rise so high that the only way he could shut her up would have been with force.

"Listen, boys, I don't have anything to lose, one way or the other, because I'm not involved," she stated loudly.

George knew that she was repeating that statement so that she would clear herself, but he didn't mind. He had taught her to look out for number one.

"Now Jay, and you too Emilio, you boys know me, so you know I don't have nothin' to lose in this matter so what I say is true. When George says he hasn't done any business with the Blacks lately he's tellin' the truth. For one reason, he hasn't got any stuff. I mean it. We have had to go across town to Mickie's to cop a blow just for me, so you know he ain't got nothing. If he had it, would he go over to Mickie's and waste his money? No, not George, and you guys know it!"

Pedro let out a laugh. "You say Mickie's, huh," he inquired, staring her in the eye.

"Sure, sure, that's who I said," Maria answered now more sure of herself.

"Would you bet your life on it?" Pedro asked sharply, his eyes never leaving her face.

"What do you mean will I bet my life on it?" Maria asked quickly, not liking the look in the young man's face.

"I mean, Maria, if we take the time to check this shit out and find out you're lying, your ass will be tied into this shit as deep as George's, because then we'll know that you lied trying to save his fuckin' worthless life!"

Maria tossed her head back, throwing the long black hair back out of her face. "Oh, yeah, I see what you mean. Of course, because I'm not lying. Yeah, go ahead and call, I'll give you the number," Maria said, full of confidence.

George wasn't as certain as she was. He hadn't missed the look that passed between the men when Mickie's name was mentioned. "Maria," he began, then caught himself, when she looked down at him. He didn't know what to say. George climbed up off the floor where he had remained ever since he got knocked down. It was better to remain down than to continue to get knocked around as long as you were on your feet.

"Don't worry," Maria said happily, sure now that she could straighten the trouble out. It was just like men to make mountains out of molehills. "Here," she yelled, as she fumbled around in her purse, "take this number and get in touch with Mickie. The quicker you call, the sooner we'll have this crap straightened out. Oh yes, ask him to get me a piece of stuff ready. I'll pick it up in a little while."

Pedro only grinned at her. He didn't bother to reach out and take the number from her hand. She stared at him surprised and before she could ask any questions, Pedro spoke to the heavy-set Jay.

"Okay, Jay, she says she's a friend of your

people so it's only fair that you do the calling,"
Pedro said, his thin face almost bursting in a grin
that only he seemed to understand.

Jay didn't seem too happy about his task. He
stared around dumbly, not wanting to look anybody in the eyes. Slowly he made his way over to
the telephone and picked up the receiver. Everybody noticed that he didn't have to ask anyone for
the number. He quickly dialed Mickie's, then spoke
into the receiver quickly.

From the look on his face, the people could tell
that he wasn't particular about the news that he
received. Jay put his hand over the receiver and
spoke to the group of people watching him.

"Mickie says he hasn't seen Fat George or his
woman in over a month," Jay said, relaying the
message that he had received.

George just stared coldly out the window. He
had already put it together. Mickie wanted his
business, so what other way was easier for him to
get it, than to allow these young punks to do what
he didn't have the nerve to do himself.

But Maria didn't take it that easy. When Jay's
words finally made sense to her, she began to yell.
"Let me speak to the lying sonofabitch," she
screamed at the top of her voice. "I can't believe
it," she continued. "It's just not possible, George."
She turned to him for the first time. The open
disbelief in her face hurt George. For the first time
he realized just how much this woman had come to

mean to him.

"Maria," he began, "don't you see what's happenin' girl? Somebody had to tell these lies on me, so who else could gain from it except Mickie. We should have seen through it sooner, that's all. I wish there was some way we could prove that sonofabitch is lying, but for the life of me, I can't!"

Pedro let out a chilling laugh. "You're right about that! It ain't no way in the world for you to prove it. Your proof just went out the goddamn door!"

"Emilio," George said, turning to the older brother, "can't you see through this shit? Listen man, I don't even need the money. I got thirty thousand dollars in that suitcase right there."

Even though they didn't want to look, every man inside the apartment glanced towards the suitcase. "With that kind of money, Emilio, don't you know I'd have to be a fool to sell some dope to them spades, man. Why, I don't love them guys, amigo, I just did business with them. Better to see them strung out than our young people, right?"

George glanced around to see if his words had made any sense. He had taken a great risk telling them about the hidden money, but it was the only way he believed he might be able to save his life.

Maria stared at him curiously. She had known about the money, yet she would have never believed George would come out and tell anybody else about it. It was their life savings, everything they had worked for was packed away in that suitcase. Even as she thought about it, she realized that their troubles would be worse than she imagined. George would never have revealed the location of the money unless their lives were at stake.

It was hard for her to accept that these young boys would really kill them. But George had panicked, and maybe that was all it was, she reasoned. Then she stopped. There was no use fooling herself if their lives were at stake.

Maria raised her head and began to scream at the top of her voice.

Pedro was the first one to reach her. He knocked her down with a vicious blow to the head, but it didn't hush her up. She covered up her head and continued to scream. "You want to rob us, that's all," she yelled up at them. "You come in here talking about selling dope to the niggers, but that's a lie. All the time you just wanted to rob us. George, you're the fool for telling them where our money was!"

A vicious kick by Pedro hushed her up. She rolled over on the floor clutching her stomach. "Next time you open your mouth, I'll kick all your teeth out!" Pedro warned.

George turned on Emilio. "Every time you came to me sick, Emilio, I never turned you down. Never," George stated, then continued, "yet you come over to my house talkin' this shit about

selling stuff to Blacks, when you know I never did.
Okay, you want to rob me, okay, now what? Take
all my money, what next? You guys going to kill
me and my wife, huh? Not because of no Blacks,
though. Let's be truthful about it, you so-called
Mexicans are just a bunch of thieves, that's all! If
you had needed money, you could have come to
me and got it, but that's not good enough! You
want it all!''

Before he could say any more, Pedro stepped up
and floored him. As he rolled over, Pedro kicked
him viciously in the face. "Now, let's quit playing
games. We want to know where you drop the dope
off for these Black studs. Okay, George, let's have
the truth. No more of this robbery crap. We came
for information on those niggers you run around
with, and we're going to get it!''

Emilio looked as if he wanted to say something
to his younger brother, but just couldn't find the
nerve. He opened his mouth to speak, but no
words came out.

Neat, well dressed Vic pushed away from the
wall. "Pedro, I don't know, man, it's not going like
we hoped. Now, there's a lot of bread in that
suitcase, man, so why don't we just pick it up and
get the hell out of here?''

Pedro whirled on him, "What the hell are you
talking about, Vic? We didn't come here like
common criminals to rob and then sneak away. We
came to make this dude talk about niggers.''

Pedro's eyes took on that faraway, wild look. "Niggers, man, that's what killed my people, Black niggers!" He whirled around on his brother.

"And you, Emilio, you should feel the same way. Nothing will make you happy but the sight of some Black niggers wallowing around on the ground trying to hold in their fuckin' guts! This is what you should be interested in, Emilio, not no fuckin' money some bastard made selling it to them Black dogs."

Emilio wiped the sweat off his brow. He didn't know what to say to his brother. In the last few days things had changed so. Now he didn't know which way was up.

"I don't know about you," Vic stated, "but I'm damn sure interested in the money!"

At the sound of his words, Maria rolled over on the floor and sat up. "See," she screamed, pointing her finger at them, "I told you bastards that it was the money that you wanted! Come in here spilling that crap about niggers when all the time you knew it was just an excuse to rob us!"

Her words seemed to drive Pedro into a rage. The young man rushed at her wildly, kicking and punching as she rolled over on the floor, trying to get out of his way. Suddenly he stopped and removed his long switchblade knife.

Maria's eyes grew large as window panes as she stared up at the wild man approaching her. "Oh my God," she gasped.

176

by Al C. Clark

As Pedro went past George, the fat man stuck out his foot and tripped the frantic young man. "Emilio," he screamed, "are you going to let your brother cut us up? Amigo, I said you can have the money, now why the bloodshed?"

"Goddamn you," Pedro screamed as he scrambled around on his knees. "I'm going to gut you, you fat bastard! You stinkin' dope selling lard of shit!" His voice rose and fell, but his intentions never wavered. He held the knife out in front of him as he crawled towards George. Before any of the shocked men could react, Pedro had reached the prone figure and plunged the knife deeply into one of George's outstretched legs. George let out a scream of pure pain as the knife went in. There was more then just pain behind his yells, there was fear for his life. He knew that the wild-eyed young man meant to kill him. His only hope now seemed to be that one of their neighbors would hear and call the police.

Maria leant her voice to the screaming. She saw the blood when Pedro brought the knife out of her man's leg. Blood gushed out onto the floor. Maria screamed over and over again. She had been hoping somehow that the noisy old woman who lived below them would hear and call the police.

Jay stepped in front of Pedro. "Pedro," he pleaded, "let's just take the money, Amigo, and split. If we should want this punk, man, we'll know where to find him."

George climbed up against the wall and leaned back. The pain in his leg was just beginning, but he could easily endure it if that was all that happened. But he was not to be that lucky. He watched as the wild-eyed Pedro shoved past Jay and regained his feet. He rushed over to George, murmuring curses under his breath. Specks of foam seemed to be forming at the corners of his mouth.

George tried to raise his feet and keep his legs in front of him. As Pedro came rushing up, George raised one of his legs and kicked out with it. Though he had never been a fighter, George realized that his life was involved now. He kicked wildly at the frantic Pedro.

Pedro avoided his leg and bent over and stabbed George twice with the knife. Each time the knife went in George let out a scream.

"Goddamn it, Emilio," Vic yelled at the top of his voice, "do something about your brother! He's blowing his fuckin' marbles!"

Emilio was too shocked by his brother's actions to react. All he could do was stand and stare at Pedro like someone watching a horror movie. He was shocked almost out of his wits!

Maria, unlike Emilio, had seen too much violence in her lifetime not to recognize insanity when she saw it. It was out of hand now, she knew. The only thing she could think of was a way out for herself. George was hurt, she didn't know how badly, but she knew it was serious. If someone didn't do something soon, she might be lying on the floor bleeding alongside George.

Watching for her chance, Maria suddenly jumped up from the floor and made her run for the door. She managed to get it open before she was caught from behind.

As Maria lunged for the door, Pedro saw her and yelled at Jay. "Take care of that lying bitch!" The order worked on the heavy-set Jay like a command. Before, as he stood filing his knife, he hadn't known what to do, but now that someone had given him a direct order, he went right into action.

Jay caught Maria from behind. As she opened the door, he grabbed her around the neck and pulled her back inside the apartment. Even though he had her neck, he didn't stop her from screaming until he got her back into the apartment. He didn't even remember sticking the long-bladed knife into her back.

When she fell back into his arms, blood gushed out of the back wound, covering his hands and arms. The checkered white jacket he wore was covered with red.

The other two men in the apartment didn't even realize that Jay had stabbed the woman until she screamed. "George, George, he's killing me." Maria yelled hysterically.

The sound of the woman's voice caused Pedro and Emilio to glance at the struggling pair by the door. What they saw would stay in their minds until the day they died. Maria tried to pull away from the pain in her back, and when she finally managed to turn and face Jay, her white blouse was completely covered with blood.

Without even knowing what he was doing, Jay continued to stab the woman. First he hit her in the chest with the knife, then he slashed downward, making a long cut on her neck. Maria slumped in his arms, but it didn't make any difference. Jay was past knowing what he was doing. He was caught up in the bloodrush of the moment.

George managed to get to his feet. As Pedro glanced around to see what his partners were doing, George struck out. He had had a glimpse of Maria and knew in his heart that they didn't stand a chance. All he wanted now was to make someone pay for what they were doing.

George's fist caught Pedro flush in the face, breaking the nose. Pedro let out a scream of pain before George struck him again. George was a fat man, but he was strong. His punches dazed the younger and smaller man.

Before Emilio could come to Pedro's rescue, George raised his foot and kicked the man in the groin. Reaching down for the falling Pedro, George grabbed the front of Pedro's shirt and brought his fist down in a crunching blow on his uplifted face.

Emilio, seeing the punishment his brother was taking, came out of his daze long enough to help.

by Al C. Clark

As he went toward the struggling pair, Vic ran around him and grabbed the suitcase. He wanted to open it, but he knew the rest of them would come to their senses before he could finish doing it.

With the suitcase under his arm, Vic rushed for the front door. He stopped in the doorway and took one more glance back at the madness going on inside the blood-spattered flat. For a second, he couldn't take his eyes off the shocking sight.

Emilio had George in a bearhug from the rear. He was pulling the enraged fat man backwards, away from his screaming brother. The stab wounds didn't seem to bother George as he made a frantic last effort to break loose and reach the man in front of him.

Pedro was whimpering like a hurt dog, while feebly wiping at the blood that came streaming down from his broken nose. As Vic watched, George managed to push backwards, slamming Emilio against the wall. The sound of the two bodies hitting the apartment wall was loud.

"Goddamn," Vic muttered over and over again. He hadn't expected anything like this to happen when Pedro had called him up and invited him to take part in the job of putting Fat George in his place. All Vic had believed would happen was that George would get a good ass kicking to teach him a lesson. Now it was beyond anyone's control.

One look at the woman on the floor was enough to tell a man that murder had been committed.

Maria lay at the feet of Jay, who was standing over her body looking stupid. He still held the knife in his huge hand, but he didn't seem to know what he had done. His face had a vacant look about it. He stared around dumbfounded.

"Oh, shit," Vic murmured, it was completely out of hand. Without another look, he pushed the door open and went out. With the money he had in the suitcase he could put a lot of miles between himself and the police. It was just a matter of time, he believed, before somebody called them up. All the noise they had made should have been reported. As Vic ran down the hallway he noticed people peeping out of their half open doors. At his approach, they quickly slammed the doors closed again, but they had had enough time to get a good look at him.

Well, it wouldn't really matter, he believed, if he was able to get away from here. Vic took the stairway three steps at a time. The large suitcase under his arm caused a little problem with his progress, but it didn't hinder him that much. Before he reached the bottom steps, the door leading to the outside flew open and two uniformed police officers came through.

Vic tried to stop instantly, but his momentum was too great. He clutched at the suitcase as he felt it slipping from his grip. By the time he had the bag firmly in his grip, he was staring into the barrels of two huge pistols.

182

"Hold it right there!" one of the officers yelled out loudly.

He might as well have remained silent for all his order meant. Vic didn't have any thoughts of giving himself up. As a picture of the mayhem in the apartment flashed through his mind, Vic whirled around on his heels and started back up the steps. He had to get away. There could be no thoughts of giving up. To surrender would mean he would be charged with murder. Even though he hadn't participated in any of the insanity that had gone down, he had been there, and that was enough to get him convicted.

"I said halt!" the officer called out at the top of his voice.

Just a few more feet, Vic prayed as he took the stairway two steps at a time on his way back up. The sound of the policemen cocking their weapons went unheard by the fleeing man as panic filled his very being. The only thing on his mind was flight, nothing else. If he could only gain the top floor he might be able to avoid the inevitable.

The sound of the pistols never reached him. He was struck in the back and lifted the rest of the way up the stairs. Vic staggered from one side of the hallway to the other, still holding tightly to the suitcase. For some reason the suitcase was important, though he couldn't think of the reason now. The weight of the bag became too heavy and he let it slip from his grip. He continued to stagger onward.

The policemen ran up the stairway in time to see Vic slowly crumpling against the wall. "Why didn't the bastard stop?" one of the officers said. "Jesus Christ, he never had a chance of getting away!"

The other officer glanced over at his partner, "Whatever he was running from, he believed it was bad enough to take a chance with his life!"

An elderly woman came out of her apartment and beckoned to the policemen. As they approached she began to speak. "I'm Mrs. Davis, I'm the one who called," she stated, as though she was entitled to a medal. When she saw the officers weren't going to say anything, she continued. "It's been going on in that apartment, right there," she stated, and pointed out Fat George's apartment. "I don't know what's going on in there, but the woman's been screaming at the top of her lungs, and its not like them folks. They're generally quiet, even though they're Mexicans. There's seldom any noise made in that apartment!"

The sound of the gunshots out in the hallway had done more to bring sanity to the men inside the apartment than anything else could have. Emilio snapped out of the dream-like state he had been in. With one well placed rabbit punch, he knocked Fat George down to his knees. Before the fat man could open his mouth, Emilio had removed a hankie from his pocket and crammed it down the fat man's throat. George continued to struggle, but another punch to the back of the neck dropped him to the floor.

Pedro had found his nerve again. He moved toward the pair of men with his knife out. Emilio reached around George and knocked the knife out of his brother's hand.

"You fool, you," Emilio snarled. "Haven't you made a good enough mess out of this shit already? Let's hope like hell Fat George doesn't die on us, you dumb bastard!"

"Like hell," Pedro growled, then quickly removed a small caliber pistol from his inside pocket. Before Emilio could reach him, Pedro had pointed the gun at the man on the floor and pulled the trigger. The sound of the small pistol going off in the apartment wasn't as loud as a fire cracker, but it was loud enough.

"Goddamn," Emilio growled, then ran toward the wide windows that looked out on the well kept grounds of the building. As he searched wildly for the window lock Emilio heard his brother open the front door of the apartment.

The sight of the young man covered with blood coming out of the apartment carrying a pistol in his right hand took both the officers by surprise.

Pedro was just as surprised to find policemen in the hallway. He panicked and began to run. There was no thought in his mind to give fight. Even though he held a pistol, he had no intention of using it.

"Drop that weapon!" one of the policemen yelled out loudly.

Pedro didn't even hear the order. He was too intent on fleeing. Before he reached the stairway both policemen had raised their weapons. One of them put a shot over Pedro's head, trying to warn him, while his partner took a more serious aim. When Pedro didn't drop the weapon and continued to run, the second policeman held his weapon in both hands and pulled the trigger.

The bullet went into Pedro's back and came out his chest. The force of the shot knocked the pistol out of Pedro's hand as he stumbled and fell, his fingers clutching at the banisters. His hand opened and closed, and then he died. The wild light in his eyes became dim, and then went out completely as the last flicker of life left the body.

Inside the apartment, Emilio heard the gunshots. They added speed to his search for a catch on the window. Not finding one, he picked up a small chair and tossed it through the glass. The sound of breaking glass was heard by the policemen.

Using the chair, Emilio knocked the rest of the glass away from the edges of the window. He didn't want to get cut when he went out the window. Emilio took another glance out the window. The jump was just two floors so it wouldn't be all that bad, he reasoned. Quickly he stuck his legs out and began to lower himself out the window.

by Al C. Clark

At the sound of the glass breaking, Jay looked up from where he stood. He still couldn't get over what had happened. It was like another person had taken over his body. He watched Emilio go out the window, wanting to run over and go with him, but for some reason he couldn't keep his eyes off the dead woman at his feet. He couldn't understand why he felt guilty for her death. It wasn't his fault.

The sudden commotion of people jamming the doorway came to Jay as though from far away. He saw the two men in blue uniforms come in, but didn't pay them any heed.

"Sonofabitch," one of the officers cursed as he took in the blood-smeared apartment. His partner had seen a man's hands on the window sill as they came rushing in. He ran towards the window.

Emilio dropped from the broken window. He landed on his feet but quickly rolled over, taking the weight of the drop off his ankles. When he regained his feet he glanced up to see a white-faced policeman leaning down pointing a pistol at him.

"Hold it right there!" the policeman yelled out. "Don't make me kill you!"

At the sound of the order Emilio froze. But as he realized what he had left behind, the idea of surrendering left his mind. He could still see Jay standing over the dead woman. There was no way he was going to give himself up for a murder charge. Taking one more quick look up at the man in the window, Emilio made up his mind. He broke to the right, first, then zig-zagged back toward his left, hoping to throw the policeman's aim off.

The first shot missed him by three feet. Emilio cut back to his right quickly, searching for the safest route. If he could only reach the parking lot, he reasoned, he'd have a good chance of getting away. Their car was parked there, and once he reached it he could be gone before the policemen could get back down the steps.

The officer in the window rested his pistol on the edge of the window frame and took dead aim, then slowly pulled the trigger. Even before he fired he knew he had missed. Emilio had cut back quickly to his left just as he fired.

Damn, the policeman cursed under his breath. He took his time and aimed again. This time he allowed the fleeing man to make his sudden cut. He waited patiently until Emilio cut back again. As soon as he was sure the man wouldn't make a sudden cut, he slowly squeezed off his next shot. He let out a grunt of satisfaction as he saw the fleeing man stumble.

Pain exploded between Emilio's shoulder blades. He knew he had been hit, but hoped it wasn't too serious. He continued to run, even though he had slowed to a crawl. The sudden appearance of a police car in front of him didn't phase him at all. He attempted to go around the car, as it stopped in front of him. The sight of a tall, pale-faced man jumping out with a pistol in his hand didn't disturb

by Al C. Clark

Emilio either.

As the policeman ran up to Emilio, Emilio felt himself beginning to fall, and couldn't determine the reason for it. He was weak, weaker than he had ever been before in his life. Suddenly the concrete came up and hit him in the face, but he was beyond feeling even that.

The darkness that slowly overcame him brought relief, his worries disappeared and a slight smile of contentment appeared on his face as death embraced him for the first and last time.

Later on more detectives arrived on the scene. The first two police who had arrived went over their story again. There was an apartment full of dead people, with one living witness who had been there, yet after talking to Jay, the policemen were still in the dark as to the reasons for the murders. The suitcase full of money had been found. At the end, of the conversation, robbery and murder was the verdict. But none of the policemen could really make any sense out of Jay's participation in the gruesome killings.

There was no doubt in their minds that he had killed the woman, even though he claimed he hadn't. But the bloody knife that he had held until some policemen had forced it from him didn't have anyone else's fingerprints on it but his.

The detectives went back over everything again, but at the end they were only sure of one thing. They had the murderers, true enough, but Jay

189

would never stand trial. The heavy-set Mexican would spend the rest of his life in an insane asylum.

13

DAN GLANCED UP AT THE SKY as he made his way back. He cursed under his breath as he turned up the collar on the light gray jacket he wore. The early evening chill was setting in, and he could feel it in his very bones. One reason for it, he believed, was because he hadn't had his fix yet. After that, he reasoned, he might be able to put up with the brisk wind.

In his hurry to reach a destination where he could fix, Dan forgot about being careful. The only thing that was on his mind was reaching a safe place, away from prying eyes. If he had taken his time and had looked back over his shoulder, he wouldn't have missed the young paperboy following him so openly.

After crossing another street, Dan stopped and reconsidered. Why waste time going all the way back to the deserted house he had left when all he had to do was find another empty house. With this in mind, he began to pay more attention to the houses he passed. After walking another block, he believed he saw just what he was looking for. It was one of the modern houses that someone had moved into, then vacated. The front of the house was boarded up, but Dan wasn't concerned about that. He was sure there was another entry to the house.

But there was one problem. If the house was completely boarded up, it would be too dark inside for him to fix his jive. He had to have enough light to see by. And then, there was always the problem of water. If he had only wanted to sleep, it would have been perfect, but he wasn't looking for a place to lay his head right now.

Dan walked past the house and noticed that there were no boards on the side windows, even though someone had gone to the trouble of putting up screens so that bricks wouldn't knock out the windows. That was cool, he reflected. If he could only get inside now, everything would be okay. There was definitely enough light inside to see by. After walking past four houses, Dan quickly cut through the first yard he saw.

His movement had been so fast that he almost took the young boy following him by surprise. The kid rode his bike up to where Dan had turned off, and laid it against the fence. He climbed off and followed quickly on foot. He was just in time to see Dan turn into the backyard of the deserted new home.

Dan walked up to the rear window and closely examined it. There was no way for him to force an entry without making any noise, so that was out. After closer scrutiny Dan noticed that the rear door could be forced, but again he didn't want to make any noise. If he had just been looking for a place to sleep, he could have kicked the door in, disregarding the noise.

Once he had the door kicked open, all he would have had to do would be leave, then return a couple of hours later. That way, if anyone had heard him kicking the door and called the police, they would have come on out and departed by the time he returned to get some sleep.

But that wasn't the case at this moment. Dan needed a place to fix, and the longer he put if off the worse he wanted the drugs.

He was so preoccupied that he didn't notice the young kid who walked past in the alley. On the boy's second pass-by, Dan still didn't see him, as he leaned his weight against the door to see just how much it would give. Under his weight, the door opened slightly, revealing that someone before him had already removed the nails from out of the bottom of the boards that made up the door.

Someone had taken the new door and all that was left were boards.

Dan glanced around quickly, then raised his foot and gave the bottom board a hard kick. The board came flying off. The noise wasn't too loud, he told himself as he nervously glanced over his shoulder. He saw a young Black boy walk past, but that didn't concern him. The boy seemed to be minding his own business, so Dan quickly forgot about him. He now had one of the boards off, and after a minute's quick work, he had another one off.

Taking another quick look around, Dan made sure the noise hadn't aroused any of the nosy housewives nearby. Then he started to slip under the loose boards. He caught himself just in time. Removing an old paper cup from his pocket, Dan came off the rear porch and walked around to the house next door. He searched the windows of the inhabited house to make sure nobody was peeping out of one of the windows at him. He moved up to the outside water spout then stuck the cup under it and filled it up with water. When he finished, he made sure the tap was turned off tight, then went back to the vacant house.

Not taking any chances, Dan set the cup of water down first, then pushed it under the door. He took another good look around, then got down on his belly and slipped under the two boards he had removed. Once inside, he stood up. He could see that someone had surely been inside. The house had been stripped of its furnishings. Someone had removed all the new cupboards. The modern sink that went with the new house was gone, and when Dan looked into the bathroom, he saw that someone had stolen the toilet and bathtub. The facebowl was also missing.

Goddamn the bastards, Dan cursed under his breath. He had removed enough furnishings from vacant houses in his life time to know just what kind of prices they brought on the market. As he searched for the room with the most light, he passed the small furnace and smiled. Whoever had ripped the house off hadn't known how to take the furnace, or didn't have anywhere to get rid of it.

Dan smiled bleakly. He knew where he could get fifty dollars for the new model furnace, but it took two men and a car to get it away. It wasn't too much of a job taking it out, but there was a little noise involved that made it risky.

Dan finally decided to do the stuff up in the kitchen, right next to where he had come in. That way, he would have the light from the door where he had removed the two boards. As he glanced down he could see from the growing shadows on the floor that he would have to move quickly or there wouldn't be enough light for him to see by. Dan rolled up his sleeve, took off his belt and tied up his arm. He ran his fingers up and down the veins, feeling for the largest one.

In a second he had the one he wanted, so he put

his dope into the wine top he had put out on the floor. Quickly he lit three matches and held them under the top. When it got too hot to hold, he shifted it to another finger, and still retaining his grip on it. The dose inside the cooker quickly dissolved.

He took the end of his dropper and slowly stirred the drugs around inside the cooker, making sure everything mixed. When he was satisfied, he leaned down and drew up some of the drugs until his dropper was full.

It took a minute, because of the dimness of the kitchen, but Dan finally got his hit. Blood rushed up into the dropper. He let out a sigh and slowly began to run the fluid back into his vein. A relaxing mood settled on him as the drugs took their effect and he settled back against the wall and nodded.

His worries disappeared, there was no fear in him now, only a contented feeling. His head dropped down on his chest and Dan closed his eyes. He could have been asleep in a large water bed from the pleased expression on his face. For the time being, Dan didn't have a care in the world.

After a decent time of waiting, Tommie, the young boy, came out of hiding and ran toward his bike. He was sure he had found Dan's hideout, now all he wanted to do was relay the message. He counted in his mind what he could do with the fifty dollar reward he would get from Rita's brother Curtis after he told him about Dan's hideout.

He thanked his lucky stars for stopping off that day and talking to Rita. He was having fun with her when Curtis walked up and asked him if he knew his friend Dan. When he said he had seen Curtis and Dan together a few times, Curtis had then offered him fifty dollars if he should ever see Dan and take the time to let him know where he was.

As the thought flashed across his mind, Tommie put on his brakes and turned around quickly. He rode back to the empty house that Dan had occupied. He quickly wrote down the address, then turned around and started riding away as fast as his bike would go.

Across town Curtis carried Shirley's bags out to the car. She didn't want to leave, but Curtis wasn't taking any chances. After what had happened, he knew either one of the Fernandez brothers would take any kind of risk to hurt him. It didn't matter who they reached either. He wished wholeheartedly that he could make his mother understand, but her understanding was zero. Nothing he said to her would make any sense. All he could do was hope that the Chicanos wouldn't strike at him there. Until he could make sure of that, he'd have to get somebody to watch the house when he wasn't around.

Shirley came out of the house herding the kids

in front of her. "I know this is just a waste of time Curt, but since you say the kids might get hurt, I'm not about to take any chances," she said as she came up to the car.

"Actions should speak louder than any words I'm able to say, girl. You see Billy is fucked up in the goddamn hospital, yet you don't want to believe me when I tell you them fuckin' Mexicans think I'm responsible for their brother's death!"

"I know, honey," she answered quickly, "but it's so damn hard to believe, it's so unfair. Since I was there, I know just what went down, so I don't see how the hell they can be so far off the track."

Curtis grinned at her as he took her arm and led her to the car door. The children jumped in the rear of the car quickly.

The drive was over almost before it had begun, Curtis pulled up in front of the modern building and got out. He came around the car and held the door open for her.

Shirley smiled up at him as she got out. "If the apartment's half as nice on the inside as it is on the outside, Curt, I might just want to stay here."

Curtis grinned down at her as she got out of the car. Even though she was his woman, he couldn't help but to look at her pretty legs as her skirt rose up around her hips as she slipped across the car seat. He grinned widely. "Shit, woman, if you don't pull your skirt down, I'll never get away from here!"

by Al C. Clark

Both of them laughed as they went up the path, leading the kids. Curtis opened the outside door with a key. "You can't even get in downstairs without a key," he informed her.

"I see it's real modern, but I'm a little worried about the inside swimming pool, Curtis. What about the children? Aren't you worried about them going near the water?"

"No," Curtis answered truthfully. "I'm not concerned with them going near the water. I am worried about them gettin' in the water though." He laughed at the look on her face. "Don't look so damn worried, Shirley. We trained the kids better than that. If we tell them to stay away from the pool unless one of us is with them, then they will do just that. Anyway," Curtis added, "they have a house rule here, children aren't allowed near the pool unless their parents are with them."

Shirley let out a sigh of relief. "Good. That's one less worry then." As they walked up the inside pathway that led to the various apartments that surrounded the swimming pool like a motel, Shirley smiled. "I see they even have a little fence up. That's real good."

"Yeah," Curtis replied as he took her arm and led her in another direction. "Our apartment is upstairs. We weren't lucky enough to get one of the ones downstairs, so we have to walk up a flight of steps." So saying, Curtis led the way upstairs. He walked around the open hallway until he reached the number he was looking for.

Curtis put the key in the lock and opened the door.

Shirley let out a squeal as she got her first look at the inside of the apartment. "Oh, Curtis, it's really lovely. I didn't expect anything like this. My God, it's like something out of a movie, Curt. Honey, what are you trying to do, spoil me?" Before he could say anything, she tossed her arms around his neck and held him tight.

For a while Curtis allowed her to embrace him, but his mind wasn't completely on it. He was too worried about his family. Billy was already one person who had been hurt because of him. He didn't want another member of his family to get hurt while he was laying up.

With slow deliberation, Curtis took her arms from around his neck. "Okay, honey, you know where that leads. And don't forget the kids are home today, too." Curtis grinned at her, as she tossed him a mock frown. Their relationship was too good to believe. That was one of the reasons why he didn't trust it. A man couldn't hope to remain as happy with a woman as he was. Something had to happen.

"Okay, Curtis, you don't have to say it, I can see it in you only too well," Shirley said. "I know, you've got to go somewhere, haven't you?"

"Now woman, I don't know why you think like that. But since you brought the matter up, yes, I think I'll make a littl' run while you unpack the suitcases."

"Oh Curt, I've got to go back down to the car, honey. I left that overnight bag on the floor in the rear of the car."

Curtis smiled at her. "Okay, girl, it ain't no problem, you come on downstairs with me. The kids will be all right here. I'll get the bag out for you and you can bring it back upstairs yourself."

"Okay," she said in a light voice. "Curtis," she said, as they started back down the stairway, "please, honey, be careful." The gun he was carrying pressed against her each time she kissed him, so it was constantly on her mind. Guns were something she was frightened of, yet her fear of them could be controlled. What she hated most was to see him carrying one. At one time it was not necessary for him to go out into the streets armed. But lately, everything had changed.

When Shirley spoke, her voice didn't reveal the fear that she felt. "Okay, Curtis, since you want to treat us mean by leaving, don't expect to find any of your favorite dishes waiting for you whenever you feel like blessing us with your company!"

Curtis just grinned at her, then opened the door and led the way out of the apartment. Neither of them spoke as they went down the stairway. Shirley was too busy admiring the rubber plants that were placed around the patio and swimming pool. They gave one the impression of the tropics.

They blended well with the natural flowers and other plants.

"Honey, how long do you think it's really going to be before you get back?" Shirley inquired as she pulled her light sweater around her shoulders. The evening was becoming chilly.

Before opening the car door, Curtis took her into his arms and kissed her slowly. There was nothing else to be said, he realized. He was only stalling. It seemed as if lately, for some reason that he couldn't understand, he hated to part from her company. Normally he hated to leave her but lately it was even worse.

"Hey, Shirley, what you doing to me? I ain't able to take care of my business for you. Here I am wantin' to go back upstairs with you, when I know all the time that I've got to get off my ass and go and take care of this business."

Shirley tugged at him, playfully trying to take him back towards the stairs. The two laughed like young children and finally broke their embrace. Curtis removed his key ring and gave her two keys. "Here, if I leave and forget to give you your keys, you'll end up being locked out!"

As she took the keys from his hand, Curtis turned and opened the car door. "Don't worry, honey, it ain't goin' be that long. Before you know it, I'll be running up the steps."

"I hope so," Shirley replied as she stepped back away from the car. She stood and watched him back the car out into the street. Even after Curtis had driven away, she stood where he had left her, staring after the car.

Curtis reached down and switched on his radio. As soon as a rock and roll number ended the news came on. Curtis didn't pay much attention to it until the announcer mentioned the shooting that had taken place on the east side of town. When the newman mentioned the housing duplex, Curtis knew at once that it involved Fat George.

The newscaster began to relate the murders, telling about the man and woman found stabbed to death and how the three Mexicans ran when police appeared on the scene. After a few seconds, the announcer mentioned the name of the couple killed.

Curtis sat straight up behind his steering wheel. He couldn't believe his ears. Why, the question exploded in his mind, why the hell would they kill Fat George? Curtis leaned over and turned the radio up louder. He didn't want to miss a word of what was being said. A slow frown of disbelief flashed across his face. This was complete madness, Curtis reflected. The killing didn't make any kind of sense.

As he listened, the radio announcer began to give out the names of the men who were believed to have been the killers. The man told that they were killed as they tried to avoid the policemen when the police tried to arrest them.

Curtis sat in stunned silence as the names came out of the radio. Emilio Fernandez, Pedro Fernandez, the broadcaster continued. But Curtis' mind was busy elsewhere now. He knew every one of the men, yet he couldn't make any sense out of it. The Fernandez brothers didn't have any reason to kill Fat George. At least he didn't think so. The men had always been fairly close friends.

The full implications of the announcement were not lost on Curtis. If both the Fernandez brothers were now dead, it took all the worry off his back. He didn't have to fear any reprisals now because there was nobody to carry out the threat. His little war with the Chicanos was over—finished.

There was no need to hide his people now. He didn't have to live in fear of something happening to them. By the same token, his friend Dan didn't have anything else to fear either. But on that score, Curtis thought he'd have to give it a little time to sink in. Think on the matter more deeper. At least now there wasn't the urgency that there had been before.

14

BEFORE HE KNEW IT, Curtis found himself parking in front of his mother's home. If it hadn't been for his sister Rita standing outside talking to a young boy on a bike, he would have pulled right back off. The last thing he actually wanted to see was his mother. He didn't want to allow her the chance of spoiling his good mood.

His tall, attractive sister beckoned to him. Curtis got out of the car and walked over to the young couple. "Hey, what it is?" he yelled out as he approached.

Rita gave him a big mouth-splitting grin. "It's a good thing you stopped by, Curt, 'cause I was just gettin' ready to try callin' you. I know hard tasks when I see one, and trying to find you over the telephone is a sure 'nuff hard task!"

Curtis laughed good-naturedly along with her, then asked seriously, "well just what is the big problem, Sis, that would take you away from your enjoyable young man here to seek me out."

"He happens to be the reason why," she answered quickly. "He said you said something 'bout a fifty dollar reward if he was to find out where Dan was and passed it on to you." She raised her eyebrows as though the message she was passing on didn't make any sense.

"Oh yeah," Curtis replied as he snapped his fingers. "Now I remember. This is our paperboy, ain't he?"

Both of the young kids quickly nodded their heads in agreement.

"Uh huh," Curtis continued. "He was here a few days ago. Yeah, that's when I told him about lettin' me know if he saw Dan. Well, young brother, from the looks of you, you got some news for me, right?"

Tommie, the young newsboy, grinned, then removed the dirty piece of paper on which he had written the address from his pocket. "Yeah, man, I seen your friend Dan go into this empty house and then I wrote the number down and came riding straight over here."

Curtis took the address out of his hand. "I wonder if he's still at this goddamn place," Curtis murmured, more under his breath than to the two kids watching him.

by Al C. Clark

"Why is Dan so important, Curt?" Rita asked sharply as she caught his eye.

"Things like this don't concern young ladies," Curtis replied slowly as he folded the paper and stuck it in his pocket.

He turned on the paperboy. "You think he's still at this place, huh?"

The paperboy answered quickly. "Uh huh. I stayed outside and watched for a while before I left and he hadn't come back out."

Without hesitating, Curtis reached in his pocket and removed his bankroll. He pulled out twenty-five dollars. "Here, I'm going to give you half of it now, and if he's still at this same place after I see him and rap with him, I'll come back by here and leave the rest of the money for you with Rita." Curtis held the money out to the boy.

The young newspaper boy grabbed the twenty-five dollars so fast that Curtis realized that he would have been happy with just that amount.

"Now don't forget, boy," Curtis added, "if he ain't there when I get there, you ain't got a god-damn thing coming, so don't wish for the impossible."

Tommie nodded his head up and down in agreement. At the moment he was wondering if it would be wise for him to come back. Suppose Dan had left, then Curtis might come back here and wait for him to show up so that he could get his twenty-five dollars back.

As Curtis watched the expressions on the kid's face, he could almost read his thoughts. He knew that he wouldn't have to put out another twenty-five dollars that evening. The boy was too happy with what he had.

"Now if you want to," Curtis said, testing the boy, "you can ride with me over to this address, and if Dan is still there I'll give you the rest of your money." As the look of greed jumped into the boy's face, Curtis added, "but if he ain't there, you goin' have to set my twenty-five dollars back out. Now do you want to ride over there with me?"

It didn't take long for the kid to make up his mind. "Naw, I'd like to go, but I got to finish up the rest of my paper route before it gets too dark." The boy was trying not to show his fear, fear of being separated from the easy twenty-five dollars he had made. He was sure then that he wouldn't be coming back looking for any more money. Half of something was a whole lot better than all of nothing.

Curtis tossed his sister a big grin, then walked swiftly towards his car. He waved back at Rita once, and noticed that the paperboy hadn't left for his route yet. If he stayed near Rita long enough, she'd con his young ass out of part of the money, Curtis thought coldly as he drove away from the curb.

It was only a few blocks away from where his mother stayed that Curtis had to go, but by the time he arrived, he noticed that it was really getting dark. He found the address without too much trouble.

Curtis parked two doors down from the vacant house, then walked slowly back to it. When he reached his destination, he walked around the house and examined it closely. He noticed where Dan had entered, but there was no way for him to tell whether or not Dan had flown the coop.

As he approached the rear door, he felt in his coat and was glad of the heavy bulge of the pistol. He stopped and wondered idly why he should waste the time going through with it. It wasn't actually Dan's fault that the Mexicans had struck at his brother. It was just one of those things that nobody could have prevented. What sat so hard on his shoulders though, was the way Dan had used him. It was hard to forget how the man had put him on front street. If Curtis would have had a weapon that night in the bar, he would have done the same thing that Ruben did.

As soon as he reached the back door he saw that the only way inside was under the boards that had been removed.

Curtis raised his voice and called out, "Hey Dan, I know you're in there. Come on out, I want to talk to you. This is Curtis, man, so come on out."

His voice fell on silence. There was no answer to his call. As he stood outside in the darkness Curtis began to wonder if Dan was really inside the vacant house. Suddenly he heard a sound from inside the building. He was sure it was made by someone moving around. The thought of Dan inside hiding from his only friend enraged Curtis. He tossed caution to the wind and got down on his knees and started under the boards.

Inside the house Dan huddled near the back door. He was so loaded that he couldn't believe Curtis had come alone. He had to have them Mexicans hidden outside somewhere, Dan believed. As soon as he had seen the shadow of the man on the back porch, he had removed his knife.

The voice came to him again. "Dan, this is Curt, man, I'm coming in."

Dan could feel his knees beginning to shake. The drugs had him so loaded that he couldn't think straight. He shook his head. Curtis' name went through his mind, but before he could really clear the cobwebs, the shadow came under the door. He saw Curtis' broad back on the floor. He reacted before giving it any more thought. He leaned down and plunged the knife into the middle of Curtis' back.

Curtis must have realized what was going on, because he instantly twisted his body, trying to get over on his stomach.

Curtis realized his error before he was under the boards. He should have slid in on his stomach, so that he could see whatever there was to see. Out of the corner of his eye, he saw something and tried to twist around. Before he could quite make it, he felt the pain explode in his back, and he knew that he had been stabbed.

"Goddamn you, Dan," Curtis cursed from the floor, as he twisted wildly, trying to escape from the plunging knife.

The sound of his name caused Dan to hesitate. He realized at the moment that he had stabbed his partner and friend. "Curt," he mumbled, as the man on the floor rolled over on his side, "man, I didn't know it was you, Curt," Dan said dumbfounded.

Whatever he said didn't matter to the man on the floor any more. Curtis had finally managed to remove his pistol from the shoulder holster. He raised up slightly and pointed the short-barreled .38 special up at the man standing over him. The first shot took Dan between the legs, blowing his nuts off. The second shot caught him high in the chest.

Not a sound escaped from Dan as the bullets struck him. The shots had taken him by surprise. As he fell back against the wall, another slug caught him, but it was a wasted bullet. The first one had done the trick. The second one only put an end to the man's suffering. Dan never even felt the third as his lifeless body began its fall.

Curtis rolled completely over and tried to stand up, but it was no use. The knife had struck him on the spine. He had no control of his legs anymore.

As he began to pull himself along, he tried to turn around and crawl back out the way he had come, but the pain was too much. He slipped into the dark pit of unconsciousness. When he awoke, it was pitch dark in the small house. The only thing he could see were two shiny little red balls that seemed to be moving around the wall.

Curtis tried to move his hands, after much effort he removed some matches from his pocket and struck one. From the light of the match, he let out a scream of pure terror. He saw Dan's body in the flame of the match, but that wasn't what frightened him. The body was covered with rats. The house had been vacant so long, that the huge alley rats had moved in. And now, they were lucky enough to find their dinner delivered to them.

At the sound of Curtis' voice, the rats scrambled away from the body. But in seconds they were back. After an hour of trying to scream at them, Curtis found his voice going. He raised the pistol and fired wildly until there were no more shells in the gun. He prayed that some one would hear the gunshots and call the police.

After another hour passed, Curtis was too shocked to feel one of the furry little rodents sniffing at his leg. He had no way of knowing how long the rats had been near his leg because there was no feeling in them.

As he lay there with the cold evening chill setting in, Curtis could feel himself growing weaker.

by Al C. Clark

He tried to fight off the sleeplessness that overcame him, but still found himself drifting off. He
instantly came awake when he felt something wet
touch his face. At once he began to beat around his
stomach and back where he could feel the blood
beginning to run freely again. Curtis felt around
until he found the matches he had dropped and
then he lit one. His first reaction was panic when
he saw the small teeth marks on his bare hands. He
realized that he had been unconscious longer than
he had thought.

With superman strength, he began to try and
pull himself back toward the door. But after a
while, he had to stop and strike a match to see if
he was going in the right direction. Panic set in
when he couldn't find the door, but after another
lit match, he saw that it was behind him. Before he
could crawl to the door he passed out again. When
he awoke he finally began to realize what he hadn't
known until that moment. Fresh blood was trickl-
ing down from his neck, and he understood why
the rats didn't run from him any more.

Now they only waited out of the reach of his
hands. Once, when he struck out at one of them,
the rat jumped on his hand and bit it. With a
scream of rage, he slammed the rodent against the
nearest wall.

It dawned on Curtis then that the huge alley rats
knew what he was just now beginning to understand. He didn't have the strength to make it. And

they planned on hindering his efforts. He started to crawl again, but this time it was useless. The crawling took all his strength. He felt the lightheadedness overcoming him again, and knew that he was about to pass out.

He glared around. It seemed as if there were thousands of eyes staring at him now. Even as the darkness rushed toward him, Curtis let out one more scream of panic. He fell into a dark oblivion so he didn't see the small furry creatures as they began their cautious approach.

Love's Fire & Glory

Fanita Moore was young, beautiful and rich. Her mother, Tallahasse Moore, had fought her way up from poverty in the South to wealth and social prominence in New York. Tallahasse adored her beautiful daughter and was determined to give her the best of everything. She had Fanita's entire future planned: the golden success and proper marriage that she envisioned for her daughter would also be the crown jewel in Tallahasse's own glorious life and career.

This is a rich and exciting story that ranges from the deep South to New York to the gilded salons of Europe between the wars. It is a story of fortunes made, squandered and regained. A story of love lost and recaptured. Above all, it is a story that will penetrate the consciousness of anyone who has ever loved, been loved, or simply dreamed of love in all its glory.

THE BLACK EXPERIENCE FROM HOLLOWAY HOUSE

★ ICEBERG SLIM

AIRTIGHT WILLIE & ME (BH031)	$2.25
NAKED SOUL OF ICEBERG SLIM (BH709)	2.75
PIMP: THE STORY OF MY LIFE (BH806)	2.95
LONG WHITE CON (BH030)	2.25
DEATH WISH (BH075)	2.25
TRICK BABY (BH807)	2.95
MAMA BLACK WIDOW (BH808)	2.95

★ DONALD GOINES

BLACK GIRL LOST (BH042)	$2.25
DADDY COOL (BH041)	2.25
ELDORADO RED (BH067)	2.25
STREET PLAYERS (BH034)	2.25
INNER CITY HOODLUM (BH033)	2.25
BLACK GANGSTER (BH028)	2.25
CRIME PARTNERS (BH029)	2.25
SWAMP MAN (BH026)	2.25
NEVER DIE ALONE (BH018)	2.25
WHITE MAN'S JUSTICE BLACK MAN'S GRIEF (BH027)	2.25
KENYATTA'S LAST HIT (BH024)	2.25
KENYATTA'S ESCAPE (BH071)	2.25
CRY REVENGE (BH069)	2.25
DEATH LIST (BH070)	2.25
WHORESON (BH046)	2.25
DOPEFIEND (BH044)	2.25
DONALD WRITES NO MORE (BH017)	2.25
(A Biography of Donald Goines by Eddie Stone)	

BOOK ORDER FORM

Dear Reader:

You'll find many other books of interest listed on previous pages. If they are not now available at your book dealer, we will be delighted to rush your order by direct mail. Fill in form below and mail with your remittance.

SPECIAL ORDER BOOK DEPT.
8060 MELROSE AVE. • LOS ANGELES, CA 90046

Please send me the following books I have listed by Number.

_____ _____ _____ _____

_____ _____ _____ _____

_____ _____ _____ _____

_____ _____ _____ _____

I enclose 50 cents additional per order to cover postage on all orders under $5.00 (California residents please add 6½ % sales tax).
Enclosed is $_____ ☐ cash, ☐ check, ☐ money order payment in full for all books ordered above (sorry no. C.O.D.'s). ☐ I am over 21

Name_____

Address_____

City _____ State _____ Zip _____
